WHISPERS WITHIN THE MIDNIGHT GARDEN

DESPERATE DISGUISE BOOK 3

TESSA COLE

Gryphon's Gate Publishing

Gryphon's Gate Publishing
550 King St. N.
PO Box 42088 Conestoga
Waterloo, ON
N2L 6K5

Print ISBN: 978-1-990587-65-8

A Quick Recap

When I took my brother Sawyer's place at the Black Tower to save his life, I'd expected my world to turn upside down.

I'd just never anticipated it would be so complicated.

My vision of Sawyer's death had become a vision of *my* death, and I knew I had the fight of my life coming.

But there was no one who'd offer me help with my training. The other guardsmen hated me. They thought I was a spoiled nobleman getting special treatment, so I tried to use that against them. If they wanted to push me around, I'd use that to become faster, more agile, and better able to take a hit.

As a noblewoman disguised as a man, I'd thought keeping my secret would be the hardest part of becoming a Black Guardsman, but I was wrong.

Every time I fell asleep, my spirit manifested in the fae's magical garden, where I appeared as a fae woman. There, I met with a fantasy man who brought me more pleasure than I'd ever known and who I was becoming attached to, despite him not telling me who he was.

On top of that, my attraction to gruff Lord Rider, kind Lord Quill, and mesmerizing Talon, just kept growing.

When Talon's shadow magic attacked me, awakening an overwhelming desire, I discovered he harbored a dangerous secret. His shadow was actually a sentient being that fed on sexual energy, and for some reason, it was particularly drawn to me.

The attack from Talon's shadow, however, made me look weaker and the other guardsmen hated me even more. And "lessons" from the group of novices who were determined to beat me down grew more violent until one of them tried to assault me.

I'd never felt so foolish or been so scared and angry in my life.

They threatened to go through with the assault if I said anything to anyone, and I'd had enough. I wasn't safe in the Black Tower and it didn't matter how much I tried to be hardworking and reliable. They were never going to accept me.

I stormed off the running trail, threatening them back that if they ever tried anything like that again, I'd kill them in their sleep.

And as a final, extremely satisfying exclamation mark to my threat, I broke Ambrose's nose.

Except Lord Rider snapped at that, and he made me run the trail until I collapsed, proving to me that even the kinder side that I'd seen of Rider, Talon, and Quill while in the Garden had been a lie.

But as much as it hurt, it couldn't matter.

The only thing that mattered was keeping my secret long enough for Sawyer to escape the Five Great Kingdoms.

Except that night, when I woke in the Garden, Wells and Crane were waiting for me, and they trapped my spirit in the Garden with a magical bracelet.

They planned to force a mating bond with them whether I wanted it or not...

CHAPTER 1
Sage

SHARP PAIN in my arm jerked me awake and my eyes snapped open. I was almost nose to nose with Wells, his lips pressed against mine, and his fingers painfully pinching the underside of my arm.

What the—?

How did I end up... wherever I'd ended up?

Then the memory of Wells and Crane cornering me in the alcove rushed through me. Just like Bramwell had easily subdued me, Crane had gotten ahold of me and I hadn't stood a chance.

Now my hands were tied above my head and Wells was pressed close. Water poured down my back, the rough surface behind me dug into my skin, and I was thigh-deep in water unable to reach the bottom with my toes.

"That's better," he purred, the look in his eyes

making my stomach churn. "You should be awake for this."

He smashed his lips against mine and painfully squeezed my breasts. Instinctually, I jerked back to evade his kiss and cracked the back of my head against the wall behind me. The sudden spike of pain made me gasp and Wells shoved his tongue into my mouth.

I heaved against his grip, my body screaming in pain from my rotation of hard labor and extra laps around the running trail in the Black Tower.

This wasn't happening. Please. First Durand? Now Wells?

I had to fight just like I had against Durand. Except I wasn't just being held. I was tied up, unable to get a hand free, and I couldn't move my legs fast enough against the water and my wet dress to kick or knee him with any kind of force. That, and he stood at just the right angle that even if I could strike, I'd only hit his thigh, and I doubt that would make him stop.

Somehow I'd gotten lucky when Durand and the others had attacked me. Ambrose had disarmed and hit me, but he'd thrown me into the stream instead of letting Durand go ahead and rape me. But now it looked like my luck had run out.

One of Wells's hands dropped and he cupped my mound, and my panic surged.

No. Please no.

I bit down on his tongue as hard as I could. The

metallic tang of blood flooded my mouth as he jerked back and slapped me, striking the bruise Ambrose had left.

My head jerked sideways and my other cheek scraped against the uneven rock behind me as stars flashed across my vision.

"Behave yourself," he snarled. "I don't like it rough. Addax does."

He stepped back, giving me a full view of the room, his arms spread wide, his grin darkly satisfied as if I were supposed to recognize where we were.

The space was a vast chamber with a ceiling that disappeared into shadows. A majestic crystal and silver chandelier with fae lights bathed the center of the room, a strange mix of temple, cave, forest, and pool, leaving the rest in darkness.

The walls were rough stone but the floor was a polished mosaic of gray, white, green, and gold tiles set in a swirling, intricate pattern. Two pillars of fae women, similar to the pillars around the courtyard, stood at the side of the pool as if welcoming those in the room to step into the water.

They were veiled, the stone so delicately carved it looked like sheer fabric, and wore flowing gowns, the hem swirling into the pool at their feet. The pink and white flowering vines that were all over the Garden curled around them and trailed over the walls and into the water, adding their soft glow to the chamber's illumination.

The water in the pool at the women's feet — and my own — undulated from the stream pouring down the rough rock behind me and reflected the soft glow from the chandelier, but held a darkness within its depth that suggested it was deep. Three steps were carved into the edge of the pool down to a platform where Wells stood — and I hung over — but I couldn't see through the water behind him and suspected the platform quickly dropped off.

Two other female statues, also veiled, stood at the entrance, their arms raised creating the arch over a dozen shallow steps leading up to... I had no idea where.

I could only presume with the statues' similarity to those in the courtyard and with the bracelet Wells had snapped around my wrist that prevented my soul from returning to my body that I was still in the Garden.

I peered into the deep shadows at the back of the chamber but couldn't tell if there was another way in or not. If by some miracle, I got a chance to run, I had to go for the obvious exit. I couldn't risk hoping there was an entranceway at the back and get cornered.

Except escaping was going to have to be one hell of a miracle because Wells wasn't the only one in the room. Lined up at the pool's edge were Crane and six other men. They were all beautiful, muscular, and tall like every fae man I'd seen so far, and they all looked at me like I was their next meal.

The biggest guy in the group had a dangerous wicked gleam in his eyes. He had to be the aforementioned Addax and everything within me yelled that he'd be worse than Edred ever was.

"I'd rather have you naked," Wells purred as his gaze raked slowly down my body, making me feel exposed and dirty. "Naked, spread wide, and tied to my bed for me to fuck whenever I feel like it."

"Stop playing with her, Wells," one of the men said. "My shift guarding the pool will be over in a couple of hours, and we don't know how long it will take for each of us to be bound to her."

Each of them?

My pulse lurched, my panic churning hard and frozen in my gut. One man who I didn't want was bad enough, but eight?

I wrenched harder against my bonds. But my wrists were bound tight and I hung from a rope looped over a chunk of rock jutting from the wall. The rock was angled up so I couldn't just work the loop off. I had to lift it first.

Except I couldn't get a good enough grip to climb up the rope, and the rock beneath my feet was scoured smooth from the waterfall and I couldn't find a foothold to lift myself up.

"I won't do it. I won't mate with you." Surely I had a

say in this. Everything I knew about the mating bonds said it was the woman who bound the men to her...

But Crane had said they had a spell.

Wells threw his head back and held up a dagger with swirling fae words carved over the blade. "The beauty of this spell is you don't have a choice."

"You can't keep me here. I'll need to return to my body," I said, guessing that if I didn't return, I'd eventually die and they wouldn't want that. What would be the point of binding their souls to mine if I was just going to die? If they just wanted to have their way with me, they wouldn't bother with the spell. "I won't tell you where I am."

"You won't have to," Crane said, jerking his thumb to the man beside him. "As soon as Thunder is bound to you, his spirit will be able to follow yours back to your body."

With a sneer, Wells swept the blade across my chest. For a second I thought he'd missed because I hadn't felt anything. Then my skin parted, the slice cutting across some of my marks and a strange green liquid that should have been blood trailed into the valley between my breasts.

The pain burst to life a second later, and Wells swiped his fingers through the strange green *blood* and watched it ooze down his fingers toward his palm.

"The eight of us have magic," he said, turning his hand and letting the light shimmer in the gold flecks caught in the green liquid. "We're entitled to a mate and we're tired of waiting and prostrating ourselves in the hopes that one of you will look at us."

He submerged his *bloody* hand in the water. Green light flickered over the pool's surface and the red light and heat in my marks flared.

"The human men don't wait for fate to give them what they want," Crane said from the edge of the pool. "They make their women obedient and they take it."

A pressure swelled around my heart and my stomach bottomed out.

It didn't matter that these men thought I was fae. I was still a thing, an object for them to take and use as they saw fit, and these men were going to treat me just like all the other men in my life had. Probably worse.

"But it would be great if you weren't obedient right away," Addax said, the gleam in his eyes darkening in anticipation.

No. Never.

My breath seized and my heart pounded, struggling against the pressure in my chest. There had to be a way out of this—

There *was* a way or I'd never have had the vision of me dead in the Gray.

Except seeing myself dead in the Gray didn't mean I wasn't also bound to these men. It only meant that my identity hadn't been discovered by the time I'd been killed... and only if these events didn't negate my vision.

I'd never had actual visions before, only a sense that something bad was going to happen. I didn't know if big events could change what I'd seen, but I was hoping they could because I was trying to change Sawyer's future.

Wells murmured something in a language I couldn't understand and brushed the blade against his fingertip. Real blood welled from the cut and he submerged it in the water.

Green light flashed over the water again and the light and heat and pressure exploded inside me. I gasped, fighting to breathe, my marks so hot it felt like my skin was burning. Tears streamed down my cheeks and the chamber started to spin.

"Please." The word slipped out and the hunger in Wells's eyes grew.

Shit.

He grabbed my face, his thumb digging into the bruise on my cheek. "Say that again."

"No." Begging never worked. It hadn't worked with Edred nor with Durand. I shouldn't have even tried.

"Say it and maybe I'll stop." But there was no remorse or uncertainty in his eyes. He wasn't going to stop. He was just playing with me. "Say 'please, *master.*'"

"No."

He slapped me again. Pain exploded in my cheek and flashes of light and darkness crashed across my vision. "Say it."

"Never."

"It's going to be so much fun to play with you," Addax said, his voice dark and dangerous and barely audible against the rushing in my head.

"Finish it," the impatient guy demanded.

Wells said more words and green light burst to life in the water and swept around him. It curled around his torso, up his neck, and down his arms. The shape of a green flower spread over his heart and sank beneath his skin, while the light around his arms contracted into bands around his biceps.

The fire and pressure inside me grew, the pain ripping a scream from my clenched jaw. It was burning me up, and I didn't know if it was because I wasn't really a fae and couldn't make soul bonds or if this was just how the spell worked.

And none of that mattered. I had to break free. I couldn't let him finish the spell. *Please no.* I didn't want to be trapped in a soul bond with him or any of them, and if they did find me in the Black Tower, all my suffering to keep Sawyer safe would be for nothing.

"No," I screamed. I refused to accept that this was my fate. It couldn't be.

I heaved on the rope, not caring that it bit into my wrists, and dug my toes into the rock behind me, desperate to find any kind of lip or crack so I could lift myself up.

Wells raised his hands, tipped his head back, and laughed. The green light around his biceps contracted into green marks, just like the marks around Lark's mates' biceps.

He yelled another word I didn't understand, and I was thrown into the center of a blazing sun. Darkness swarmed my vision and I fought to stay conscious. If I passed out, I was done for.

CHAPTER 2
Sage

SOMEONE SCREAMED, and I struggled to clear my vision. Wells had turned away from me, his body tense, the green light around his biceps pulsing in time with my pounding heart. Then he roared and pointed at—

Lord Quill?

I strained to focus through the pain and growing darkness.

It *was* Lord Quill. He had a sword and was fighting the shortest of my unwanted would-be mates.

A few feet beside him was Talon. He fought with two more of my unwanted would-be mates, Impatient Guy and a slightly taller man with black hair. Talon fought with a longsword as well as his shadow magic — or was that his shadow?

The shadow lashed out at Impatient Guy, and he

slashed through it with his dagger and lunged at Talon, who had just blocked a strike from Black Hair.

Before I could open my mouth to warn him, he sidestepped the strike as if he had eyes in the back of his head and adjusted his position so that they were both in front of him.

Behind Talon and Quill, by the shallow steps at the entrance, was an enormous wolf almost the size of a horse. It snarled and charged at Addax, but the large fae punched the air in front of him with both hands. Two fist-sized rocks shot from the wall beside me, showering me with water, and flew toward the wolf.

The wolf leaped out of the way, the movement unnatural for the beast, and its form turned smoky as if it were about to vanish. But instead of disappearing like Rider had when I'd asked him to show me around the Garden, the smoky wolf changed into Rider.

He barreled toward Addax and drew his sword, the movement fluid with no hesitation between wolf-form and fae-form.

Addax punched the air again and more rock exploded from the wall and shot toward Rider. He dodged one, but let the other skim his arm, choosing to take the glancing blow in order to close the distance between them.

Wells hissed another word in the language I didn't understand and wrenched back to face me, his eyes wild.

The pressure and power inside me surged again, and I heaved and twisted.

I. Would. Not. Be. His. Mate.

I wasn't going to be anyone's mate. Ever.

My feet scrabbled on the smooth rock and my dress tangled around my legs as Wells said the word over and over again as if that would speed up the process.

The heat and pressure in my chest grew, and I fought to keep breathing. Something hard and heavy tangled around my heart, binding me to Wells, and I knew if I didn't stop it, didn't break free, I'd be stuck with him forever.

Another of my unwanted would-be mates screamed, drawing my wavering attention to the statues at the pool's edge. A man with loose, shoulder-length brown hair who I didn't recognize — and couldn't get a good look at because his back was turned to me — fought against two more men while another lay bleeding on the ground a few feet away.

The man deftly dodged sword strikes and punches, as if he were dancing, and lashed out, drawing screams and blood even though it didn't look like he had anything in his hands... which meant he was armed with knives and knew how to use them.

More chunks of rock shot from the wall behind me, one slicing across my cheek with stinging pain that helped clear some of the darkness threatening to overwhelm me. Part of the waterfall now poured over me, pushing me down, threatening to drown me, and making my shoulders scream with the unwanted stretch.

I sputtered and gasped, fighting to get my head out of the water, but couldn't lean far enough.

Another scream and Wells snarled and jerked back to the fight.

I twisted my wrists, praying the water would help me slip free, but the rope only cut deeper into my skin.

Then another chunk of rock tore from the wall behind me, and the piece I'd been hanging off broke free.

I fell forward into the pool and out of the stream of the waterfall. Fire and pressure squeezed my insides and from the pulsing, radiating glow around Wells's biceps and the solidity of the magic wrapped around my heart, the spell creating the fake bond between us was about to be complete.

"No!" I screamed and I threw myself at Wells.

I rammed my fists into his kidney with as much force as I could muster — which wasn't as much as I wanted with my sore body and the spell threatening my consciousness.

Wells wrenched around, unmoved by my strike. Surprise flashed across his expression when he realized I'd broken free but was quickly replaced with a satisfied sneer. "You can't stop this. The spell's already done."

"It won't work if you're dead," I spat back at him.

He threw his head back and laughed. "And how are you going to do that? Do you have a powerful magic or something?"

Light flickered from his fingers and for a second I was blinded, surrounded by a brilliant white light. A large hand wrapped around my throat and hauled me off my feet, and the light vanished.

"Let's see your magic," Wells laughed, his face a breath from mine.

His fingers squeezed, blocking off my air, and I clawed at his hand and wrist. My feet were still in water so I couldn't kick him, and punching him in the face wouldn't do anything.

But that didn't mean I couldn't strike a vital point.

"I don't need magic," I gasped, and I rammed my fist into his throat.

He reared back and stumbled up the steps farther out of the water.

"You Goddess damned bitch," he snarled, and he tossed me away.

I rolled through the shallow water, my shoulder scraping against the rock, and landed face down at the platform's edge.

With a groan, I heaved myself to my feet. I couldn't stay lying down, as much as my aching body begged for it. I was still about to be soul bonded with a monster, and I refused to just accept my fate.

My experience in the Black Tower had been horrible, but I'd still gotten a taste of freedom. I'd been able to fight like I wanted and could look a man in the eyes without fear of reprisal.

I refused to go back to what I was before.

Talon's shadows latched onto Wells, turning him away from me. But more brilliant light flared from Wells's hands, burning through the darkness, and then whips of light wrapped around Talon as Wells stalked toward him, the ritual dagger raised to strike.

I lurched forward as Wells's hand darted forward, aiming for Talon's gut. Talon's shadow wrenched the blade out of Wells's grip, tossing the weapon a few inches away from me as Wells's light slammed into Talon and threw him across the chamber.

More light blazed from Wells's palms, and I could sense the power building to a dangerous level. I had no idea how I knew that, perhaps it was our unwanted connection, but I knew if the light hit Talon he'd be seriously hurt.

With a scream, I seized the magical dagger and lunged at Wells.

I wrapped one arm around his throat and slammed the blade into his back, grateful that the rope that had made me helpless hanging in the waterfall now gave me enough range of motion to strike with my full strength.

Wells roared with pain and heaved forward, but I hung on tight, refusing to let go.

I was *not* going to be bound to him. I'd rather die first.

Which meant I had to die, or he did. And I was damn well going to make sure it was him.

He straightened, grabbed a handful of my hair, and yanked, hard. Pain bit into my scalp and I gritted my teeth.

The pressure and heat from the bonding spell burned so hot I feared I was going to burn up, and the light around Wells's new marks flared. The certainty of the bond locked into place around my heart, and I screamed.

No!

Shadows, no!

With a wail, I jerked the dagger free and plunged it back into Wells. I did it again and again, aiming for his heart. I refused to be his. I refused to be any man's possession.

Blood poured from Wells's back and he screamed in agony.

Then the light from the glowing green bands around Wells's biceps exploded outward, ripped my grip free from his neck and the dagger, and I flew through the air away from him.

The soul bond squeezing my heart vanished, and the bands around Wells's arms disappeared. I hit the back wall of the cavern, the force smashing my head against the rock and stealing my breath, and dark spots flooded my vision.

With a splash, I tumbled into the pool, sinking lower and lower and lower. Above me, through my wavering vision, light rippled over the top of the water. Everything grew muffled and far away, and all the fight I'd had within me, all the anger and fear and determination to not become Wells's mate, rushed out of me, leaving me weak and exhausted.

I tried to kick up, tried to swim to the surface, but I couldn't make my arms or legs move. Everything hurt too much. Just thinking about moving hurt, probably because my head roared with agony.

The spots in my vision grew, turning the flickering illumination above me into a narrow strip of light. This was it. I wasn't going to die in the Gray. I was going to die in some pool in the fae's magical garden.

Except I was in my spirit form here, trapped in this form by the magical bracelet Wells had snapped around my wrist. Which meant technically, I was also going to die in the Gray, in my bed.

I wonder how long it will take for someone to find me?

I prayed it was after the two days of lieu time. But that was still too soon. Sawyer needed more time.

The water swirled around me and my eyes flickered open for a moment. Above me, the most beautiful, heartbreaking angel, swam toward me, his face split between fae beauty and horrible scars. His shoulder-length dark hair billowed around him while fear filled his eyes and I reached for him, welcoming him to my embrace.

If I was going to die, it was fitting the angel who'd come to take me to the heavens was a mix of the divine and sorrow.

I wanted the divine so desperately, wanted to find peace and acceptance for who I really was.

And yet who I was spelled sorrow for me in the world I lived in. According to everything I'd been taught, what I wanted was an abomination, an ugly red scar on my soul, just like the scar on my angel's face.

CHAPTER 3
Rider

RED TINTED my vision and an overwhelming rage I'd never felt before roared through me. My wolf howled at me to save her, to kill anyone who got in my way.

Goddess above, I should have never left her to fend for herself in the Garden. I knew she was unsteady, knew she was shy, and I'd abandoned her. And now—!

The fury consuming me tore a howl from my throat that roared through the sacred pool's chamber and drew terrified glances from the men closest to me. And they should be afraid. They'd hurt what was mine and they would pay.

The power pulsing from the mating bands around Wells's biceps exploded, and Sage flew through the air. She slammed against the back wall of the sacred chamber and dropped into the pool's deep water. I lurched toward her, but Addax shot another fist-sized chunk of rock at my head, forcing me to jerk out of the way.

Fuck. Fuck fuck fuck.

I wouldn't be able to save her until I'd dealt with Addax, and the asshole didn't seem to care that three of the men who were in the chamber with him to do Goddess-knew-what to Sage were already dead.

Just die already.

With a snarl, I lunged toward him, twisting out of the way of another rock as well as his fists, and managed, somehow, to slide my longsword into the man's gut instead of lopping off his head. He screamed, his eyes wide with surprise as if the idiot thought I wouldn't hurt him — or maybe because he'd expected me to kill him.

But as much as I wanted to tear him to pieces — *needed* to tear him to pieces — I needed him alive more. Someone needed to live so the Knights of the Order of the Sacred Grove, the men who protected the High Priestess and the Garden, could interrogate him.

At first glance, it had looked like they were going to torture Sage and the Goddess had started to bond her with Wells to protect her, but then Sage had broken free, fought Wells, and stabbed him to death — something she wouldn't have been able to do if they were destined to be mates.

Addax turned to smoke and vanished, his soul returning to his body. But it didn't matter where he was. He hadn't kept his identity a secret and the Order would track him down.

That, and the man would wake with a bleeding hole in his torso, since wounds taken in the Garden while in spirit form manifested on your physical body when you returned.

With Addax gone and Wells lying lifeless in a puddle of blood, I raced to the sacred pool to save Sage. It had taken me seconds to stab Addax, but it only took seconds to drown, and it looked like Sage had hit her head on the rock wall.

But before I could reach the edge of the water, Ash was already diving in. I wrenched my gaze back to the chamber, despite my wolf's insistence that we jump in with him.

Sage was small for a fae woman. Ash wouldn't have any trouble rescuing her. Better to ensure the rest of the chamber was safe.

Goddess, she *had* to be safe.

Talon and Quill were breathing heavily, but the rest of the chamber was empty. Four men were dead: Wells, Brooks, and two more who I didn't recognize. Which meant Addax wasn't the only one who'd gotten away. Wells never did anything without Crane, and Ash had said Crane had used his magic to make Sage pass out when they took her.

Thank the Goddess we'd arrived in time.

Although we shouldn't have needed to arrive at all. She should have been by my side—

No. Fuck no.

She shouldn't have been with me. She wasn't mine. She wasn't my mate. I wasn't ever going to replace Isemay.

As we had planned for our evening, Quill, Talon, and I had headed to the concert hall to meet my sister and her mates for our annual celebration of the new novices in the Black Guard... who weren't really worth celebrating this year.

The novices at the Black Tower were a mess, Sawyer, our youngest and smallest guardsman, was a mess — mostly because of me — and I was on the verge of losing it. I'd been furious, my wolf barely under control, and I'd been praying Lark, with her magic to communicate with animals, would be able to calm my beast. Because I sure as shit wasn't able to.

But before we'd even met with Lark and her mates, Ash, who we'd thought had returned to the Black Tower, found us and said Wells and Crane had abducted the new redheaded arrival.

Quill had gone ahead to the concert hall and told Lark we needed to leave, and we sent our spirits to the sacred grove where I shifted into my wolf and tracked Wells to the sacred pool's chamber.

My anger surged stronger. I should have been there to protect her. I knew Wells and Crane were interested in her. They'd made that clear when they'd asked me if I was courting her.

Except I'd been pissed at her for lying, just like Amber had lied about us courting, thinking Sage was trying to trap me into mating her.

I refused to be tricked or manipulated like that. I didn't want a mate. I'd already met my soul's mate and lost her. I refused to take another — and my wolf could shut the fuck up about Sage being ours.

But I also knew how unsteady Sage had been, how shy she seemed. If she really was as shy as Isemay had been, she wouldn't have confronted Wells and Crane. She would have deflected.

She would have used me as a shield.

Shadows! I'd fucked that up by telling Wells and Crane I wasn't pursuing her. This attack was my fault.

Ash emerged from the water with a gasp, set Sage on the smooth, wide, shallow steps rising out of the sacred pool, and rolled her to her side. All of her mating marks pulsed an angry red, no sign of gray marks indicating she'd completed the bond with Wells and had lost her mate.

Quill fell to his knees beside her. "She's not breathing."

My wolf heaved, straining to take over. She *had* to be breathing. She just had to.

"Pound on her back. Get the water out," Talon said

as he knelt beside Quill, his shadow writhing over his skin.

"I know," Ash snapped, giving her three sharp palm strikes.

"Harder," my wolf snarled, and I dropped beside them and cut through the rope tied around her wrists with my claws.

Her face was turning blue and I refused to accept her death. Fury pounded through me. How dare they! How dare Wells and his cronies do whatever they did to her?

Her wrists were bleeding from where the rope had cut her, her left cheek was dark red and swelling, and a small pool of blood had formed on the rocky floor beneath her head.

This shouldn't have happened. Women were precious.

This woman was precious.

I'd known Wells was trouble, but I never thought he or anyone would take a woman by force and hurt her.

Ash struck again and she coughed, spitting up water. Quill leaned forward, cupping her cheeks, holding her head steady so she didn't knock it against the stone floor, and her eyelashes fluttered but her eyes didn't open.

"She needs medical attention," Quill said, moving to take her from Ash.

But Ash drew her to his chest, making Quill's eyes widen in surprise.

Shit.

This was going to get complicated, and not just because I couldn't stop thinking about Sage or that my wolf wanted to yank her from Ash's arms and protect her.

I'd thought Ash seeing Wells and Crane abduct Sage had been happenstance, that he'd decided to do other business in the Garden before returning his spirit to his body in the Black Tower.

But if he wasn't just handing her over to Quill like he usually would, it looked like there was more going on with him. I had no idea what, although I doubted he'd actually talked with her. When it came to women, he was as bad as me. Except the difference between us was that I didn't want a mate and he did.

"We need to get her someplace safe," he replied, his voice thick with an anger that matched my own.

"And we need to tell the Order what happened," Talon added, his body tense as black smoky tendrils curled down his forearms, reaching and withdrawing toward Sage. They didn't touch her, but it seemed like they wanted to, and he was barely managing to hold them back.

And it said something to the fury racing through me— hell, to the state we were all in that none of us reacted to the allure that had to be pouring off Talon while he struggled to control his shadow.

With a groan, Talon heaved the shadow back under his skin and jerked his chin toward the sacred chambers entrance.

"There's a conception suite nearby with a hidden entrance and soundproofing," Talon said. "We can get a healer to her there."

Ash narrowed his eyes. "How do you know about the suite?"

"Let's just say some of my lovers don't want others to know I top them," Talon replied.

That, and Talon didn't want others to know that *I* topped *him*. Only Quill and Ash had known we were lovers when the shadow had first infected him, but neither of them had witnessed us fucking. Talon liked being dominant, but no one dominated me, and back then, he'd needed to fuck. I was an alpha among the fae who possessed an animal form, and I wouldn't accept submitting to anyone.

"Let's go," I said.

We'd been in the sacred pool's chamber long enough. Someone was going to show up and if it was the Order of the Sacred Grove, I didn't want Sage involved in the interrogation until I knew she was all right... if I was going to let them near her at all.

CHAPTER 4
Rider

THE OTHERS FOLLOWED me out of the sacred pool's chamber, Ash still clinging to Sage as if his life, and maybe hers, depended on it.

Would he work up the courage to talk to her? If Sage was the woman I thought she was — which was only my instincts because I hadn't spend time to get to know her — she wouldn't dismiss Ash because of his scars.

He would protect her, I told myself. I wouldn't be necessary if she had Ash.

Except my wolf hated that idea. She could have an army of men at her side, but he wouldn't be satisfied if he wasn't there, too.

"We also need to be careful who in the Order we go to," Quill said quietly as we hurried through the winding passages in the sacred grove, the white and pink glowing flowers illuminating our way.

"I agree," Talon said. "There should have been someone on guard in the chamber. We don't know who to trust."

"We have to trust someone," I growled, frustrated that Talon was right while trying to convince my instincts that I was right, too. "The sacred pool's chamber has been damaged and defiled, and at least four fae have been killed in their physical form. We can't keep her hidden from this."

"We sure as hell can," Ash snarled.

We reached a dead end where the flowering vines thinned against a stone wall, and Talon reached into the thicker foliage at the edge of the wall and pressed the button that opened the hidden door.

"She was attacked. She deserves justice," Quill said as we strode inside.

The hidden chamber hadn't changed in the hundred years since Talon and I had last been there, and because of the magic in the Garden, everything was clean and pristine, even if the room hadn't been used in a while.

The space consisted of three rooms, the first being a comfortable, cozy sitting room with soft couches and chairs, thick rugs, and pillows. A fire burst to life in the hearth, and two of the six lights in the chamber brightened, casting a soft, warm glow around the room.

But none of us stopped in the sitting room and we all headed to the bedroom.

"I also want to know why she didn't just release her spirit form and escape." Ash laid Sage on the large, soft bed.

Quill sat on the bed beside her and lifted her arm to examine an intricately wrought silver bracelet around her forearm.

"It's the bracelet," he said. "This word here is for lock and this is for spirit." He pointed to small words engraved along the edge. "It must be keeping her spirit form locked in the Garden."

"Who the fuck would make something like that?" I growled.

"It looks like an artifact," Quill said. "If it is, I doubt even the magisters know who made it." His expression darkened. "But no one in the White Tower has said an artifact is missing."

"Which means it might not just be the Order we have to worry about," Ash replied, his voice dark.

A growl rumbled in my chest, and my spirit form trembled. My wolf strained to break free, hunt down the rest of the men who'd attacked Sage, and tear them to pieces. But the man in me knew we needed to be smart about this.

"Our first priority is a healer and someone who can take off that bracelet," I said as Talon ran to the bathing room and grabbed towels from the rack just inside the door.

"Also she needs someone to look at her marks," Quill added. "They shouldn't be this bright when she's unconscious."

"I don't know what Wells was doing, but of the ones in the room that I recognized, all of them were unmated." Talon brought the towels to the bed, where Ash grabbed two, slid one beneath her head, and placed the other across the relatively shallow gash along the top of her chest. "Everyone we get to help needs to be a woman or mated."

"Agreed." I leveled my gaze on him. "Talon, get Onyx. We need to report what's happened to the Order and he's high enough in rank to get things done. Lark will understand if we need to borrow her mate."

"Lark will ask questions," Talon warned as he wrapped one of Sage's wrists in a towel.

Ash wrapped her other wrist. It was cumbersome, but it would slow the bleeding until we could get her a healer. "Bring Lark, too."

My wolf heaved and fur rolled over my hands and forearms. "No. I'm not getting my sister involved in this. It's too dangerous."

"Red needs someone she can talk to and it can't be us," Ash insisted.

"Why not?" Talon demanded and Ash glared at him.

"She was afraid of Wells and Crane and the other unmated males before this," Ash replied. "She might be worse when she wakes."

Another growl slipped free. "How do you know that?"

Talon's eyes widened as he stared at Ash. "You've spent time with her."

The muscles in Ash's jaw flexed and he hesitated, his gaze locked on Sage's too-pale face, his body rigid. "Anyone with eyes can see she's afraid of males. She made a point of avoiding them. Rider, you're the only one she seems to have said more than a few words to, and she hasn't been back to the courtyard since her first night."

Maybe he'd done more than just watch her... although everything he'd said could have been learned through careful observation, something he was skilled at.

Except, I'd never seen him react to a woman like this. It gave me hope that perhaps the Goddess would bind their souls together, and he could finally forgive himself for that horrible night.

But that wouldn't happen if we didn't take care of her.

Shit. Every instinct I had screamed to keep Lark out of this... and to stay with Sage and protect her. But protecting her would give her the wrong idea, and I didn't want to make things worse.

"We'll involve Lark if absolutely necessary," I said. "Let's see how Sage is when she wakes. Quill, Flint can't heal spirits but Zinnia can. Get her and a mated magister you trust to deal with the bracelet and her marks."

Everyone's attention jerked to me.

"You know her name?" Talon asked. "No one knows her name. That's been the talk throughout the Garden since she arrived."

"She told me when we first met," I growled back. "I asked. Maybe the rest of the men need to stop seeing her as a thing and start treating her like a person."

"She wouldn't have let anyone get close enough to ask," Ash said, his voice soft. "Afraid of the men, remember."

"But not afraid of you." Quill tilted his head to the side, examining me. "Will you look after her?"

"No," I bit out as my wolf strained to say yes. "I don't want a mate. I'm not here to court her. I'm going back to the sacred pool to get everyone's scent and look for clues about what they were doing." I turned my attention to Ash as he pulled two blankets from the chest at the foot of the bed and covered her with one of them despite the fact that her dress was still wet, while leaving the second one folded at her feet in case she wanted it when she woke.

I opened my mouth to tell him to get her out of her wet clothes first but stopped myself. If she really was afraid of men, waking naked would only scare her more.

"You stay here," I told Ash, "and keep watch."

Ash jerked to his feet. "I can't."

I bit my tongue against trying to convince him that maybe this time would be different. I didn't know if it would be, and even if I did, he wouldn't believe me.

If it hadn't been a woman who'd broken his heart so completely by looking at him with horror, gasping, and gossiping, I would have beaten up everyone who'd hurt him. He was already punishing himself. It was plain to see with his scars manifesting on his spirit form. He didn't need anyone else making it worse.

"Someone needs to stay," I told him. "Her marks are too bright. If she wakes and Talon's here, his shadow will overwhelm her."

"And the last thing she needs is being caught up in his allure," Quill said. "You could probably find Zinnia, but you're not as familiar with the White Tower magisters as I am, and we need to be careful who we bring in on this."

"Between the four of us, you're the best at close quarter fighting." I placed a hand on his shoulder, drawing his attention away from Sage.

"No," he bit back. "She'll be terrified of me."

"Ash, please." I *needed* him to protect her. My wolf wouldn't rest easy— *I* wouldn't rest easy, unless I knew she was safe while I hunted down everyone who'd hurt her.

CHAPTER 5
Sage

GROGGY AND DISORIENTED, I struggled to make sense of the voices around me, but throbbing pain radiated throughout my body along with a burning, aching, desperate need that made it difficult to focus.

"...know her name?" Talon asked, his voice right beside me.

I tensed as Lord Rider growled a response that I couldn't make out.

They were so close and I lay—

My pulse roared, panic rushing through me. Had they discovered the truth? I was waking up from... something, and they surrounded me. I had to be in my room in the Black Tower.

Oh, Great Father. Please, don't let them know my secret. Not yet. Sawyer still needed time, and I wasn't ready for whatever punishment Rider was going to give me when he learned the truth.

I'd thought I could trust them, but after Lord Rider had made me run the trail until I'd thrown up and Quill and Talon had turned their backs on me without even glancing my way, I knew the truth. They didn't care. As Sawyer, I was a nuisance. As Sage the girl, I was nothing.

"...stay here and watch," Rider said.

"I can't," an all-too familiar voice said, making my thoughts lurch.

Why was Fantasy Man here? He wasn't in the Black Tower... at least I didn't think he was. He was in the Garden.

My thoughts lurched again.

The Garden. I'd been in the Garden, and Wells and Crane had attacked me, tied me up, and tried to force a mate bond on me.

My breathing picked up. I'd almost been mate bonded to Wells, and then I'd stabbed him until the forming bond shattered.

I'd killed him.

I'd murdered two men now, and the horror bubbled up inside me even as I knew I'd do it again if I had to.

"...last thing she needs is being caught..." Quill said, yanking my wavering attention back to the guys.

"Between the four of us, you're the best at close quarter fighting," Rider added.

I didn't understand why they'd saved me. They'd wanted nothing to do with me in the Garden before, and yet all three of them had shown up to rescue me.

"No," Fantasy Man said, his voice strained.

He must have been the fourth man I'd seen in the pool chamber and now he didn't want to protect me.

The thought hurt worse than the pain radiating through my body, and I couldn't understand why. I barely knew him. We hadn't shared our names. We'd just had sex a few times. And yet I'd always felt safe with him. I'd trusted him like I'd trusted Talon and Quill in the Black Tower.

Of course, I'd been completely wrong about Talon and Quill. I was probably wrong about my Fantasy Man.

"She'll be terrified of me," Fantasy Man added.

"Ash, please," Rider growled.

A whimper escaped my throat as my desire surged stronger. He didn't want me. And I was the idiot girl who wanted him.

"She's waking," Rider said. "We should leave so we don't frighten her. Keep her safe, Ash."

My eyelids fluttered open, and I caught a glimpse of three large figures hurrying toward a bright entranceway. Another figure stepped away from me, sinking into the shadows of the dimly lit room.

He had to be Ash, my Fantasy Man... who didn't want to stay.

No. He thought he'd terrify me.

He dipped his head, allowing his jaw-length hair to fall forward, obscuring the right side of his face.

"You're safe," Ash said, his voice sliding over me like it always did, sending shivers of longing racing down my spine. "You're in a conception chamber in the Sacred Grove."

Father! I ached for him like I'd never ached for anyone before. Even those times in the Garden when I thought my desire was unbearable were nothing compared to the burning, twisting need pounding through me now.

Except that wasn't really me. It was the spell Wells had used to form a mate bond between us.

It had to be.

A fae woman's mating marks compelled her to have sex when it was time for her to find her mates, and somehow, even though I couldn't possibly be fae, I had the marks. That had to be why my body was going crazy, why my need was so much stronger than the pain pounding in my head or rippling through my body every time I even thought about moving.

"I promise," Ash said, keeping his distance in the shadows. "No one will hurt you."

Which was what I'd originally believed when I'd

talked to Kit and Payne. Fae men respected their women. Fae women were revered.

But that wasn't true. Wells and Crane had attacked and hurt me.

I curled into a ball, fighting to keep my desire contained while also trying to make myself as small as possible. My body screamed for sex, but my soul screamed for me to hide. I wasn't safe anywhere. I hadn't been safe in the Black Tower before Durand had tried to rape me, and now I wasn't safe in the Garden.

My throat tightened and my eyes burned with tears. I wanted to be strong. I really did. But I was terrified. Would Mikel and his friends attack me again? Would other guardsmen? How long could I possibly keep my ruse up? I wasn't as strong as a man, and I was foolish to think I could pretend to be one. And now the Garden—

"Hey," Ash said softly as he drew closer and picked up a blanket from the foot of the bed, but stopped before reaching me, the shadows and his hair still hiding most of his face.

His hesitation made my soul weep. I needed him. The thought was irrational, but I couldn't stop the ache squeezing around my heart.

"Please." I held out a hand, urging him to come closer, begging him to wrap me in his arms like he had when we'd cuddled on the couch in that secret nook and stared at the stars. "I won't look. I promise." I swallowed at the painful lump forming in my throat. "I know there isn't anything between us, but..."

Ash's grip on the blanket tightened. "I'll scare you."

"You won't," I insisted. "You fought those men to protect me. Please, I need—"

My desire surged, dragging a moan from my lips.

"It's not— I can't give you that." But he took another step closer. "Your marks are too bright. We'll be bonded, and you don't want me as a mate."

I didn't want anyone as a mate. I wanted to be free, able to make my own decisions, and not be beholden to any man. But if I had to be stuck with someone, it'd be all right if it was Ash, my Fantasy Man. He was the only man who'd ever made me feel safe.

Except I wasn't even fae. I shouldn't be showing up in the Garden every night. Would my soul even bond with his?

Maybe we could have tonight, and he'd ease the yearning burning inside me and make me feel wanted.

No! There was still a chance we could bond. Only fae were allowed within the Garden and yet I'd woken up here every night since I'd stepped into the Gray. I couldn't risk it.

I'd sacrificed everything for Sawyer, and I couldn't forget the vision that had convinced me to take his place in the Black Guard. I wouldn't lose my only remaining family member to the Gray. I had to keep going.

Except it was so hard. I was already worn thin, and I'd only been at the Black Tower for a single rotation.

Tears rolled down my cheeks. I just needed someone, anyone, even for a moment, to care.

"Please," I choked out, reaching out for him as my need surged stronger. "I need—"

"I know, Red." Ash's shoulders sagged. "I know. You'll learn my name soon enough and know the truth," he murmured.

He inched closer and I realized, even in the dim light and with his hair hiding half of his face, that he was the heartbreaking angel who'd pulled me out of the water — the one with the horrible scar covering the right half of his face.

"You saved me," I whispered.

He brushed a hand through his hair, pulling back the strands and offering a brief glimpse of the sorrow I knew lay beneath. His image was already burned into my soul the moment he dove into the water and reached for me.

Pain twisted the unblemished side of his face, but I knew it wasn't physical. This was why he'd said he'd terrify me. He thought he was hideous, thought I'd run from him screaming. Was that how others had behaved?

It broke my heart thinking a man who'd shown me

such kindness and care had people who treated him with disgust all because of a physical injury.

I knew disgusting, horrible people, and Ash couldn't compare. He was nothing like my step-father, Edred, who'd beaten me and Sawyer for no reason, or Wells and Crane who thought they could force themselves on me. Even Durand thought he had the right to take what he wanted from me.

My chest tightened, the memories flooding in, overwhelming my desire and pain. I had no safe place to go. The fae men in the Garden were just as bad as the human men who owned me.

Be strong. Please, I had to be strong.

But I couldn't breathe, couldn't push back the overwhelming fear. I was going to die in the Gray and there wasn't anything I could do about it.

"Hey," Ash said softly, finally shuffling up the side of the bed and wrapping the blanket around me. "It'll be all right. I've got you."

He pulled me close, my back against his chest. My desire spiked, but I wrapped my arms around myself, resisting the urge to respond to my body's yearnings. I needed his comfort more than I needed sex, but I wasn't sure how long I could resist my burning mating marks.

CHAPTER 6
Ash

SAGE TREMBLED IN MY ARMS, both blankets now wrapped tightly around her slight frame, though it did little to ease her shivering. Her long, dark red hair hung limp and damp, and my heart clenched as I looked down at her tear-stained face.

Her usually vibrant emerald eyes were dull with shock. I couldn't believe she hadn't been repulsed by my scars. Every woman and half of the men who'd seen me since that horrible night had been. And yet all Sage wanted was for me to hold her.

It had to be shock, not to mention the compulsion burning in her too-bright mating marks. Once she calmed down, she'd act like everyone else.

The thought made me want to scream at Wells for hurting her and at myself for getting attached. I shouldn't have gone ahead with my ridiculous plan to spend time with her without her seeing me. I shouldn't have searched her out again and again.

I knew eventually everything would come crashing down, and now it had.

Except if I hadn't been compelled to look for her, I would have never known what had happened. I wouldn't have been there to protect her.

Goddess above! I couldn't get the image of Sage hanging half under the small waterfall that fed the sacred pool out of my head.

I shouldn't have wasted time getting the other guys. I should have jumped Wells and Crane the minute I saw Crane use his magic to drain Sage's strength and make her pass out.

But while Wells's and Crane's magic wasn't as strong as Quill's or Rider's — or even mine given the right situation — it was strong enough that I wasn't certain I'd win a two against one fight with them. And if something had happened to me, no one would have known what they'd done.

As much as I hated it, getting backup was the better call. I'd thought because she was a precious female, they'd just keep her captive. I certainly hadn't expected them to torture her.

My anger boiled hot and fierce. She was so shy to begin with, so uncertain about her place in the Garden.

Now she was going to be terrified of everyone. It

didn't matter that she'd somehow become an amazing fierce survivor and killed Wells. From our conversation on the balcony above the courtyard, I knew stabbing Wells to death would haunt her... even if he deserved it.

I drew her closer and tightened my embrace. The movement shifted the blanket a bit, exposing some of the brilliant red marks encircling her neck and trailing into her cleavage.

Her mating marks had been fully awakened when we'd first met, and her desire had seemed overwhelming. It was one of the many reasons I should have stayed far away from her.

But the connection when we joined had been addictive. Seeing her shy uncertainty, her need... it had compelled me to be with her.

Now her mating marks blazed bright against her pale skin, so much brighter than before, telling me in no uncertain terms, that even if she wasn't repulsed by me, I couldn't continue to be with her. The chance that the Goddess would bond our souls together was too strong.

My traitorous cock hardened, and I shifted to hide my obvious desire. I had to focus on comforting her, not on how her marks would drive her to desperation and how much I wanted to feel the connection we formed when I was inside her again and again.

"I just," she said with a hiccupping sob as she

nuzzled her face into my neck. "I just need to stay strong. Stay strong."

"You are strong," I murmured against her temple.

Each sob tore at my heart. Sage was sweet, gentle, and brave. She deserved protection, not the chaos that had been thrust upon her. I wanted to shield her from the world, cradle her like this forever, but I knew I wasn't enough. I was broken, scarred both inside and out.

I stroked her hair, my emotions churning as she started to rub against me like a cat. Every fiber of my being craved her, ached to give her the release she needed. But if I gave in now, with her marks so bright...

No.

She wouldn't want to be bonded with someone like me. Once the shock wore off, she'd realize how hideous I truly was. She'd want nothing to do with me.

"I tried so hard," Sage whimpered. "But I-I can't. I'm not strong enough. I don't belong here."

"You do. You are strong enough. And you're safe now," I said, cupping her face in my hands to meet her gaze. "No one will hurt you again."

Her eyes finally focused on mine, brimming with fresh tears. "You can't promise that. You don't know, you— I can't be here. I can't—"

My chest tightened at the pain and fear in her voice. But the harsh truth was that it didn't matter what she wanted. Sage couldn't avoid the Garden. It was the only place fae women could find their mates and conceive. No matter how much she might want to run, this was her destiny.

I opened my mouth to offer more reassurances, but the words died on my tongue as Sage squirmed closer. Her hips rocked against my leg, seeking friction, and I bit back a groan. The pressure from her mating marks was clearly building, and I was hard as steel.

She pressed lingering kisses up my throat and across my jaw, seeking my mouth. The mating marks on her skin blazed brighter, bathing the room in a red ethereal glow, their compulsion growing stronger by the second.

A breathy moan escaped her lips and she turned in my arms and straddled me. Her hot core pressed against my cock, the heat blazing through my pants, and red hot need shot through my veins. I grabbed her by the hips to stop their movement and clenched my jaw.

"You don't want this," I gritted out, trying to gently nudge her off me and back onto the bed.

"I know," Sage whispered. Shock no longer dulled her eyes, now they were glazed with need.

"We could end up mated," I warned, desperately clinging to the last shreds of my self-control.

"I don't want a mate." The words were barely out of her mouth before she ground down on my hardened length.

My eyes rolled back and I bit back a moan. *Fuck, fuck, fuck.*

My hands slid to her shoulders of their own accord, and my fingers slipped inside the neckline of her dress, brushing against her feverish skin.

She moaned, the sound vibrating against my cheek, sweet and raw. Then she rolled her hips again, and the heat of her core threatened to unravel what little restraint I had left.

"We can't do this," I growled, even as my body screamed for more.

A whimper escaped her lips and she stilled, her entire body trembling with the effort. Strain etched her expression, and her breathing turned into short, sharp gasps. She wouldn't be able to hold out much longer. The compulsion from the mating marks was too strong.

I had to take control of the situation before we did something she'd regret. Even without intercourse, there was still a chance we could end up mated. But I had to do something to ease her suffering.

With a growl of frustration, I rolled us over, pressing Sage into the mattress. I hovered above her, our faces inches apart. My gaze searched hers, looking for any sign of revulsion at my appearance. But all I saw was an aching, desperate hunger that matched my own.

My heart raced as I dipped my gaze down to her

soft lips, slightly parted, as if inviting me in. This might be the only chance I'd ever get to kiss her face to face.

We'd shared hard, needy kisses before when I'd been able to control which of my cheeks brushed against hers. But there was something more intimate about being able to fully see each other, to look her in the eyes and show her how I felt. Kissing face to face for us was about more than playing together and having sex.

It was, at least for me, a confession.

Slowly, giving her every opportunity to push me away, I lowered my mouth to hers.

The first brush of our lips was soft, tender. Just the barest whisper of contact, and Sage's moan of pleasure sent a shiver down my spine.

I deepened the kiss, urgency taking over, her taste intoxicating, soft and sweet. With a low groan, I teased the seam of her lips with my tongue until she opened for me.

I raked my tongue against hers, and, as if that gave her permission, she let go. She kissed me back with fervent need, her hands grasping at my hair and pulling me closer, deeper, as if she were afraid I might pull away.

The heat radiating from her was almost unbearable, her need lighting the conception room as if we were outside in the middle of a sunny day.

I slid my hand down the inside of her dress, teasing

my fingers across her breast, deliberately avoiding her nipple and drawing a whimper. Her fingers dug into my scalp and her hips bucked forward, dragging her heat over my rock-hard cock.

Oh, fuck me.

I wanted to give her everything, to unleash the need driving both of us crazy. But even in this moment, when my instincts screamed for me to take her, I had to stay in control.

With my jaw clenched tight against my screaming desires, I brushed her nipple with my thumb. I had to drive her crazy, get her to the edge and make her crash over it again and again if I had any hope of easing the pressure from her mating marks.

Sage gasped and arched her back, thrusting her breasts up.

"More. Please. Harder."

She tipped her head back, exposing her pale throat, and I trailed my lips along her jaw and down to her neck, savoring the way she shivered beneath my touch.

"Please," she begged, her voice breaking with need.

I had to give her relief. Even if I couldn't be inside her, I could still help her reach the release she so desperately craved until Quill returned.

Without magic, he was the only one who could safely have sex with her without risking a mating bond... or at least he was the only one she might actually want to be with. She could have sex with any of the men she was afraid of and a bond wouldn't form, but that would just be cruel.

No, it had to be Quill. When we'd talked on the balcony overlooking the courtyard, she'd said Quill had looked kind, and he was. He was exactly what she needed right now: someone kind and caring who wouldn't bond with her. She deserved to choose who she mated with, not end up with someone because her marks had gone crazy and she didn't know what she was doing.

And I needed to give her enough relief for her to hold on for his return. No matter how much it killed me to not connect with her.

Determined to maintain my control, I pulled down the shoulders of her dress, exposing her breasts to the cool air. My pulse pounded, my need screaming inside me, as I leaned closer and flicked my tongue across her nipple while kneading her other breast with my hand.

I watched her reaction, captivated and smugly satisfied by the way she responded to my touch. Unlike anyone else, she'd gifted me her trust. It was a heady thing, and even though I wasn't buried inside her, I could feel the tingling heat of the magical connection I made with a fae woman teasing along my veins.

Every noise she made shot straight to my cock. But I couldn't keep both of us on the edge. It would be too easy to lose control, and I forced myself to keep my focus, to remind myself why I was doing this.

I released her breast and shifted down the bed, shoving the damp blankets out of the way. Sage's confused whimper quickly turned to a gasp as I kissed her inner thigh, urging her legs further apart.

With a groan, I settled between her thighs, dropping kisses up her sensitive skin and inching her damp dress higher and higher until I reached her center.

Her hips rocked faster, driven by need. The light from her mating marks blazed so bright it was hard to look at her.

"Please." She grabbed handfuls of my hair and tugged, urging me closer to where she needed me most.

The heat of my magical connection flared stronger, overwhelming me, and I dove in to taste her with broad sweeps of my tongue, unable to stop myself.

I licked and sucked with a frenzy, barely clinging to any kind of control. Sage gasped and moaned, her hips rocking faster and faster.

With a cry, she arched off the bed, her muscles contracting and sweet release flooded over my tongue. Her moans sang through me, entwining with the tingling heat of my impossible magical connection with her.

But I couldn't let up. Not now. One orgasm wasn't enough with the kind of light and heat radiating from her marks. The only way to ease the pressure was to completely exhaust her.

I lapped at her cum, relentlessly driving her through her orgasm and building another one. My cock screamed for release, desperate to be buried inside her.

With a strength of will I didn't know I possessed, I shoved my hand down my pants and quickly jerked myself off, hard and fast, coming with her second, gasping orgasm. Then I grabbed her hips and doubled my assault, determined to make her marks and her body succumb to my will.

CHAPTER 7
Talon

THE DIMLY LIT passage outside the hidden conception suite stretched before me as my shadow writhed beneath my skin with a rage more powerful than I'd ever felt before.

Somehow it had kept itself contained when we'd rushed the red-haired new arrival to the hidden suite, pulling itself and its allure into a tight ball around the spark in my heart. But the minute I'd stepped back into the passage, it had roared to life, exploding from within me with dark, writhing lashes of shadow. The force of its rage was so strong, I had to press my shoulder against the vine-covered wall to keep standing.

I didn't understand its reaction. I knew why *I* was furious. No man should ever attack a woman and certainly shouldn't tie her up and do whatever the hell

Wells had done to her. But my shadow didn't have the same sense of morals as I did. Hell, I didn't even know if it knew what morals were.

For the longest while, it seemed like my shadow only had base emotions: hunger, contentment, rage. But its repertoire of feelings had grown over the years, suggesting it was more than just a base, mindless creature.

It felt sympathy and frustration over my love for Quill and my decision not to ask him to bond with me. And when we'd seen the new arrival, Sage, it had recognized her or something within her, and I'd been flooded with a confusing ball of emotions while it squeezed itself so tight inside me not even a flicker of allure oozed from my body.

Now I burned with a rage unlike one I'd ever experienced before that consumed all underlying feelings my shadow might have.

I hear you, I thought to my shadow even though we communicated through emotions and not words. *I want to kill every last man who thought they could hurt her, too.*

But that would have to wait. Rider was a better tracker than me, and my job was to protect Sage from the uproar that was sure to follow the moment the fae nobility learned the attack happened in the sacred pool. Not to mention protect her from anyone in the Order who'd been involved.

And to do that, I needed my shadow to calm the fuck down. I couldn't go to Onyx to ask for help with my shadow billowing from my body and releasing an ocean of allure.

We need to do this for Sage. Please.

Surprisingly, it snapped back under my skin and curled into a tight ball in my chest without any more begging. Its rage still sizzled through my veins, but I got the feeling it understood what I needed to do and wasn't going to get in my way.

Thank the Goddess.

I couldn't afford for people to ask questions. It didn't matter that I could brush it off as my magical ability to control darkness. It looked like my control had slipped, and I could be detained until I proved I had my magic under control.

And right now would be a terrible time to be detained. I needed to help protect the new red-haired arrival. Even if my honor as a fae man didn't demand it, my shadow did.

Grateful it was going to help me, I manifested in the antechamber outside the smaller of the Garden's two concert halls. The room was wide with a soaring ceiling, vine-covered window and door arches, intricately carved wooden walls, and a polished stone floor.

Ahead of me stood the elaborately carved doors leading into the concert hall where we — Rider, Quill, and I — were supposed to have joined Lark and her mates for the concert.

A haunting melody drifted from within, lutes and shawms weaving together in perfect harmony and striking a chord deep inside me, making my chest ache with hunger and longing. They were playing Quill's favorite song. The same one that had been playing the moment I realized I was in love with him.

I shoved that emotion aside and opened one of the doors to the concert hall. I couldn't afford to feel sorry for myself on top of all the other emotions raging through me. I had to focus on the job at hand: protecting Sage.

The door led to a dimly lit hall that ran along the back of the concert hall to stop light from the antechamber disturbing the performance. I hurried to the archway at the end and stepped into the chamber. Five hundred seats, only half full, sat in neat rows on a gently sloped floor facing a three-foot high stage at the front. Like many of the proper rooms in the Garden, the space was carved half from the living wood of the massive tree at the Garden's heart, and half from stone created by an Earth Master able to manipulate the earth with his magic.

I scanned the crowd and found Lark and her mates near the back surrounded by a bunch of empty seats that they'd most likely held for me and the others in case we wanted to join them.

A part of me wished we could join them. Rider certainly needed time with his sister. His wolf had been on edge before Wells and Crane had attacked Sage, and it would be a miracle if the beast let Rider transform back into a human after he searched the sacred pool's chamber for the attackers' scents.

But joining Lark and her mates meant abandoning Sage, and there was no way in hell I was going to do that.

The music swelled and Dale, one of Lark's mates and the leader of the quartet on stage, broke into a quick-paced swirl of notes on his lute with the kind of fingering that awed even his fellow professionals.

I hurried down the aisle while the music was louder and slipped into a seat behind Onyx. The song ended, everyone clapped, and two of the musicians switched instruments for the next song. I leaned forward and caught Onyx's eye.

"I need your help," I whispered, drawing Lark, Flint, and Blaze's attention as well. "Garden business."

Blaze's eyes narrowed and he wrapped a protective arm across Lark's shoulders. If we hadn't had the relationship we did, I'd have been hurt by his need to protect his mate from me. But I knew the tiger shifter couldn't help himself. He was almost as strong an alpha as Rider and his possessiveness, while a little higher than normal for a fae with an alpha animal form, was expected.

The muscles in Onyx's jaw flexed as Lark raised her eyebrows. I could see the questions in her eyes and I prayed she wouldn't ask. Rider didn't want his sister involved and I really didn't want to piss Rider off right now.

"Garden business?" Flint asked. It was his night off as the primary healer in the Black Tower but I knew he'd send his spirit back to his body in a flash if we needed him.

"Just the Garden," I said.

Dale started another song with two strong chords followed by the rest of the musicians.

"I don't want to disturb the concert." I gave Onyx a pointed look.

"Outside," he hissed.

He turned to Lark and kissed her then stood and followed me back into the grand antechamber.

"This better be good. Lark needs me right now." He turned back to the intricately carved doors, heartache flickering through his expression.

"It didn't take?" *Shit.*

Lark had been so hopeful only a few days ago. The High Priestess had blessed the sacred pool, and Lark and her mates had spent her entire conception cycle trying to get pregnant. Unlike humans, fae woman could feel the spark of a new life within them almost immediately. Unfortunately also unlike humans, it was hard for fae to get pregnant, and Lark had been trying for decades.

"It is what it is," Onyx said. "We love her regardless, but if you can take this to someone else, I'd appreciate it."

"I wish I could." I glanced around the antechamber to make sure no one was eavesdropping. "Have you heard about the new arrival?"

Onyx gave a tight nod. "Lark said she met her. Says she's sweet. She was surprised to find Rider talking to her."

I huffed. I was surprised Rider had talked to her long enough to get her name. The only time I'd come across them together, I'd scared her away so she wouldn't get caught up in my shadow's allure, and I doubted he'd had enough time to catch her name then.

Which meant he had to have talked to her at least another time. It would also explain why he'd been obsessively looking at that bench while we were having our meeting about the novices in the Black Tower.

"Her name is Sage. Wells, Crane, and a bunch of other men attacked her." I met his gaze. "In the sacred pool."

"They what?" Onyx's frustration from being taken away from his mate turned to fury. He was a Knight Captain in the Order of the Sacred Grove, and he took his job of protecting the Garden and the High Priestess seriously. "That shouldn't have been possible. Someone should have been on duty."

"Which is why I've come to you," I said. "I can trust you."

"And you don't know who else in the Order you can trust." He smoothed a hand over his long, black hair, his gaze unfocused telling me his thoughts were whirling. "Maybe it was dereliction of duty."

"Maybe. But I still don't trust a random knight to interview her. If she was shy to begin with she might be terrified of people now, especially unmated men."

"Of course." Onyx straightened his back, and his shirt and pants turned into his green, gold, and white knight uniform telling me he was only here in the Garden in his spirit form. "Take me to her. Does she need medical attention?"

"Quill's got that covered," I replied. "We've got her in a conception room. Meet you at the entrance to the grove."

Onyx nodded and his body turned to smoke as he sent his spirit to the entrance to the Sacred Grove. I closed my eyes, imagined myself there, and manifested beside Onyx in front of the arched entranceway, then we strode into the maze-like passages, the softly glowing flowers lighting our way.

"If it wasn't dereliction of duty..." Onyx said.

I could feel the weight of what he left unspoken.

The knight order was supposed to protect the Garden and those within it.

Had it just been one knight who'd turned a blind eye or — Goddess-forbid — participated in attacking Sage? Or did it go deeper than that? Someone had stopped Sage from sending her spirit back into her body by trapping her with an artifact. Was that something members of the Order knew about? It was a pretty handy tool if you wanted to hold onto a criminal's spirit long enough to retrieve their physical body.

We reached the dead-end hall and the secret entrance to the hidden conception room. I reached to push the catch and open the door but stopped and turned to Onyx.

"Ash says she's been avoiding the courtyard and thinks the men make her nervous," I said, trying to reiterate my point that she could be terrified of him.

The rage and seriousness in his eyes softened. "I understand."

CHAPTER 8
Talon

I PUSHED OPEN THE DOOR, and Onyx and I stepped into the sitting room. No one sat on the couches or chairs and the door to the bedroom stood half open. Nothing looked disturbed, which meant Rider and Quill had yet to return and Sage was still safe. If her remaining attackers had found her, there would have been signs of a struggle.

"She's in the bedroom, resting," I told Onyx. And it looked like Ash was still in there as well.

I wonder if he's still hiding in the shadows, scaring her.

Onyx eased the door open and stood back, allowing me to enter first, but my gaze landed on Sage and Ash, and I froze.

Ash wasn't hiding at all. He sat propped up by pillows against the headboard, holding Sage in a protective embrace. Her vibrant red hair spilled over both of them as her head jerked toward the door, her emerald eyes wide with fear.

"It's just Talon," Ash murmured, his grip around her tightening. "He's a friend of mine. He helped rescue you. You can trust him."

She rested her head back against his pec but kept a wary eye on me. I couldn't blame her. I'd been rude to her, and she had no reason to trust me, but I was glad to see she had a spark and wasn't cowering from me.

That spark had to have been what propelled her to stab Wells over and over again until the newly forming mating bond shattered.

My shadow curled tighter within me even as a sliver of pride unfurled in my chest. It didn't want this woman to know it existed, and it certainly didn't want its allure affecting her, but it was still proud of her... or was that my pride?

Unlike human women, fae women were strong and confident. But I wasn't sure how many of them would have had the strength to handle being strung up, cut, and half drowned, and then attack a man easily twice her size.

"I brought my friend Onyx," I told her, keeping my voice low and steady, trying not to let my anger at her attack bleed through. "He's a Knight Captain in the Order, and he'd like to know what happened. Can he talk to you?"

Sage's gaze darted to Onyx and her eyes narrowed.

"He's safe as well," Ash said. She turned her full attention to him with nothing in her expression indicating that she was afraid of the horrible scars on his face. "He's mated to Rider's sister and I trust him."

She turned back to me and nodded, and I stepped to the side, keeping my distance from her and letting Onyx enter.

He took one step forward, his movement slow and deliberate, then stopped. "May I approach?"

A flicker of surprise flashed through her eyes as if she hadn't expected him to ask for permission to get closer to her. "Yes."

"Talon tells me you've been through something terrible," he said, carefully drawing closer and crouching beside the bed. "I know this will be tough, but can you tell me what happened?"

"I woke up in the Garden again," she said, her voice heartbreakingly soft and uncertain. "I keep waking up here and I don't want to."

Her eyes grew glassy, and my shadow's rage spiked at her distress, releasing a burst of allure. She gasped and light flared from her already too-bright mating marks.

Shit. I couldn't stay here.

My shadow's regret at momentarily losing control swept through me, but I couldn't afford for that to happen again. With her marks as bright as they were, she had to be desperate for a sexual release, and my allure would only make it worse.

"Excuse me," I muttered.

I stepped back into the sitting room, partially shutting the door behind me.

Fucking hell. I needed to pull my shit together. If I couldn't, Rider would force me to leave. But my shadow wouldn't let me abandon her.

I sank onto the couch near the fire, planning to wait until Onyx was done, but couldn't sit still and jerked back to my feet. Sucking in deep breaths in an attempt to steady the emotions whirling inside me, I paced to the outside door then to the partially open bedroom door and back again.

I was on my thirtieth circuit — the room wasn't that big — when the door to the rest of the grove opened and Rider strode in, his expression grim.

His gaze darted around the room, landing on the partially open bedroom door.

"Did Lark ask questions?" he asked. He didn't bother asking about Onyx, since with his enhanced smell and hearing he could scent the man and hear him talking with Sage.

"No. But you know she's going to the moment she gets you cornered."

He huffed a sigh. "Hopefully by then we'll have this mess cleaned up. Although..."

That didn't sound good.

"I found eight different scents in the sacred pool." He glanced at the bedroom door again and sat in one of the over-stuffed chairs near the fire. "Two of them don't match the bodies we found and I didn't recognize them."

Well, shit.

Rider's wolf was strong. Not only could he smell scents in his spirit form, he could also smell spirit scents. But if the scents didn't match the dead and Rider didn't recognize them, we'd never be able to figure out who they were.

The odds that Rider would randomly catch a whiff of them were low, especially since his body was in the Black Tower and fae could only manifest in the Garden, nowhere else in the fae realm. And if I were one of the idiots that attacked Sage, I'd avoid the Garden for at least a decade.

To make matters worse, sometimes a person had a different scent in their spirit form than their physical form. Which meant he could be a member of the Black Guard, we could work with him every day, and not know he'd committed one of the worst crimes possible.

"I didn't get a good look at all of the bodies. Were any of them knights?" Onyx could discreetly find out who was supposed to be guarding the pool, but I wanted answers now and learning there were two assailants we couldn't identify only made that need stronger.

"I didn't see anyone wearing a uniform during the fight," Rider said. "And none of the bodies were in uniform, either. But we both know that doesn't mean much."

"Yeah." I resumed my pacing, unable to stand still. "They could have ditched the uniforms before joining Wells. Or..."

"Or Wells took out whoever was supposed to be guarding the pool and hid the body," Rider finished grimly.

And once again I was hit with the staggering implications. Wells could have murdered a knight, or one of the knights could have been involved. But it could also have been many knights or powerful magisters involved.

Rider got up and quietly strode to the bedroom doorway. I watched his face as he peered inside, trying to gauge the situation with how Sage was and how Rider felt about her.

"How is she?" I asked when his expression stayed typically stoic.

"Shaken," he replied as he headed back to his chair. "But Ash is still with her. Did you know they're cuddling?"

"Hard to believe, I know." Which was an understatement. Ash had hidden from all women the minute his body had healed enough that his spirit could manifest in the Garden.

The muscles in Rider's jaw flexed. "Do you think she's his mate?" he growled... or quite possibly his *wolf* growled.

I didn't know. But from his tone it sure sounded like she was *Rider's* mate.

Which didn't mean she also couldn't be Ash's.

Goddess, I hoped she was. Ash deserved happiness and that connection he craved to balance his soul.

I prayed he didn't get in his own way. As soon as the rush from saving Sage and the need to protect and comfort her vanished, I had no doubt he'd retreat. I had to make sure he gave her a chance and not let him assume she'd be terrified and disgusted by him once she was past the shock of the attack.

Of course if she *was* disgusted and afraid— If they weren't mates—

She'd shatter him.

CHAPTER 9
Sage

I SNUGGLED AGAINST ASH, trying to focus on the warmth and comfort of his strong arms around me instead of the smoldering heat burning low in my belly and around my neck.

Despite Ash giving me so many climaxes I'd passed out, the need from my mating marks was still strong, and I ached for him to touch me and kiss me again.

Beside us, Onyx sat on a cushioned stool next to the bed, waiting for me to tell him what had happened. His expression remained soft, and I got the impression he was willing to wait for however long it took for me to tell my story.

And while I recognized him from when I'd watched him with Lark and her other mates having sex, that didn't mean I knew him. He could react in so many different ways and many of them not good. Sure, fae women were supposed to be considered precious by fae men, but I now knew firsthand that was a lie.

Of everyone here, the only person I could trust was Ash.

I didn't know why. I barely knew him. Hell, I'd just learned his name. But every time he held me, I felt safe.

"So you woke up tied and hanging in the sacred pool's chamber?" Onyx asked. "And they hit you?" His gaze slid to my cheek.

It still throbbed from Wells's attack... and Ambrose's punch. A bruise on top of a bruise. A reminder that I wasn't safe anywhere.

I swallowed back the churning mix of fear and anger as best I could. I needed to stay as calm as possible. If I let go of my emotions in front of Onyx, he could call me hysterical and say I was making everything up or that I asked for it.

Which was why I was surprised Talon had brought any kind of authority, let alone a knight captain, to hear what had happened.

In the human realm, no one would have cared. They'd only have cared if their property had been damaged.

"He had a dagger and was doing a ritual that would force me to bond with him," I said, my voice trembling with my emotions despite my attempts to hold them back.

Fury filled Onyx's gaze and I shrank back against Ash's chest.

I should have kept my mouth shut. I'd thought he wanted to know the truth, but Wells could have been an important person and I'd just accused him of something horrible... at least I thought it was something horrible. Maybe Onyx was mad at me for wasting his time.

I squeezed my eyes shut. I had to stay calm and in control. I could do this. I had to.

But the feeling of helplessness washed over me. The same helplessness I'd felt hanging in front of Wells. The same helplessness I'd felt when Durand and the others had attacked me on the running trail.

"She killed Wells before the bond could form," Ash said, making me cringe.

"Good," Onyx growled. "The bastard deserved it."

"We killed a few others," Ash added. "But some got away." He lifted my arm, revealing the bracelet. "This is keeping her soul trapped in the Garden."

"That looks like an artifact." Onyx's anger bled into worry.

I could practically hear his thoughts. They were the same thoughts I was desperately trying not to think. Did anyone know how to free me? Would my physical body ever wake up?

I was asleep in the Black Tower and someone

would eventually find me. All my hard work and suffering to protect Sawyer would be wasted.

"Quill is looking for a magister," Ash said.

"Good." Onyx turned back to me. "Is there anyone I can get for you while we wait for the magister? A friend? Someone from your family?"

"Ah...." I wasn't sure what to say. If I was really fae, I'd have a large family with multiple fathers and a ton of uncles. "No. I don't—"

Shit, I had to tell him something he'd believe.

I'd told Lord Rider I didn't have anyone, and while he didn't press the issue, I doubted he fully believed me. Would Onyx believe me?

"They're not in the Garden and they're not close enough for you to get in time," I lied.

Please don't let Lord Rider and Ash compare notes about my family.

"I see," Onyx replied, doubt creeping into his tone. "Once the artifact has been removed, you should stay out of the Garden until we arrest everyone involved. I know it'll be difficult with your strong marks, but it's for your own safety."

Except I had no control over coming to the Garden.

"We can teach you to control your spirit form," Ash said, his voice soft as if he knew what I'd just been thinking. "Even if you go to sleep and wake up here, you'll be able to send your spirit back whenever you want."

Great Father, I hoped that was true.

"Just one more question and then we're done," Onyx said. "We know Wells and Crane attacked you. Can you describe any of the other men involved? Would you be able to recognize them?"

I shook my head. "I only knew Wells and Crane." It had been hard to concentrate past Wells and the dagger on top of trying to find a way to escape while knowing I was helpless. "They called someone Addax." I shivered at the memory of the man's dark expression and how he'd wanted to hurt me. "And another of them Thunder. But I didn't really get a good look at anyone. Including Wells and Crane, I think there were eight of them."

"That's helpful. Thank you." Onyx stood, his tall frame looming over the bed. "Now I need to borrow Ash for a moment, if that's all right?"

My stomach clenched. I knew what that meant.

They were going to talk about me behind my back.

Of course that was the way things were. Women had no say in their lives. They were slaves to the whims of whichever man or men had control over them. Even in the fae's realm it seemed women didn't have full control of their lives.

Except I didn't want to sit around and wait for them to tell me they'd captured whoever had gotten away.

I swallowed back a bitter laugh.

One rotation as a man and I wanted things I wasn't supposed to want and couldn't have.

Soon it would all come tumbling down and the chains I'd been born into as a human woman would chafe more than they ever did before.

It would be easier to just let them have their conversation and do what they were going to do. I wasn't fae. I wasn't supposed to be in the Garden. If I spoke up, I'd draw even more attention to myself.

And yet I couldn't stand the thought that Onyx might just be trying to appease me and nothing else was going to happen. Even if Ash taught me how to control my spirit form, I wasn't sure I'd be able to stop myself from waking in the Garden every night.

And with the ability to send myself back... It could turn into a never ending loop of forcing my spirit back into my body and waking in the Garden again. All night long.

I also didn't know if Crane was one of the men who'd been killed or caught. If I kept showing up in the Garden, Crane and anyone else who'd gotten away could attack me again. Or they could try to force a bond on another woman.

I didn't want what happened to me to happen to someone else. I, at least, had weapons training and, when given the chance, could fight back. I had no idea if fae women were allowed to become swordsmen. I'd never heard any of the minstrels' tales mentioning a female fae warrior, and something so scandalous was sure to have made it into song.

No. As much as I wanted to huddle against Ash and cry, I couldn't afford to let them have their conversation without me. At the very least, by asking to participate, I'd know if they were brushing me off and that I was on my own for figuring out how to keep myself safe.

Ash grabbed my hips to move me to the side so he could get up, but I grabbed his wrists, stopping him.

"I want to be a part of the investigation." I held my breath and waited for their dismissal.

CHAPTER 10
Sage

"I don't think—" Onyx shot a worried glance at Ash.

And there it was.

"Talking about what happened could upset you," Ash said, his voice soft as concern filled his gaze. It was clear he didn't want to leave me out, but he also wanted to protect me.

"Not knowing will upset me more." I brushed my fingers along the unscarred side of his jaw. It was just a whisper of a touch, but it drew a flash of longing in his eyes. "I need to know how many men are still out there and who I should be wary of."

In truth, I was wary of everyone. Ash was the only one who made me feel safe. And while in the beginning I thought I could trust Lord Quill and Talon, they'd proven they'd do whatever Rider said.

And Lord Rider... I definitely didn't trust him.

"All right," Onyx said, surprising me with his agreement. "I'll call Talon to join us since he's already involved in this."

Onyx strode to the bedroom door, leaving it wide open. "Can you guys come in here?"

Guys.

Plural. That meant it wasn't just Talon who was going to step into the room.

My stomach churned at the thought of facing Lord Rider again after he'd made me run the trail until I threw up. I wasn't even sure how I felt about Lord Quill. But Lords Rider, Talon, and Quill had come to my rescue. They were all involved in what had happened and I wasn't going to be able to avoid them.

Onyx returned to his stool as footsteps approached, and I braced myself for Lord Rider's glare.

Talon entered first, and, as always, I was struck by his otherworldly beauty. His long white hair seemed to shimmer and the delicate gold earring capping his pointed ear glinted in the soft fae light. I fell into the mesmerizing swirl of his pink, purple, blue, and gold eyes, and the heat in my mating marks flared so strong a moan bubbled in my throat.

I bit it back but couldn't stop the memory of his magic— or rather the memory of the magic of the shadow trapped within him from rushing through me. Hot and achy. Desperate yearning desire.

Lord Rider stepped up behind him, and a chill

snapped through my remembered need. He was taller than Talon and his chest broader. His shoulder-length black hair was half tied back in a topknot which only emphasized his rugged beauty, the three silvery scars that slashed across his cheek, the intense look in his silver eyes... and his scowl.

Swell.

Onyx opened his mouth to say something but the door in the sitting room, the one on the far side of the room, opened, and a woman entered with Quill behind her

The woman had long golden hair that shimmered like Quill's as if she were perpetually in sunlight. It was woven into a complicated hairstyle that was mostly twisted and plaited on her head with a few long tendrils curling over her pale blue robes.

Then the woman stepped aside, revealing all of Quill, and everything within me stalled. My breath caught in my throat and his gaze locked with mine, drawing me deeper and deeper into his emerald eyes.

Great Father. It didn't matter that I knew he'd do whatever Lord Rider told him. The compulsion to look at him, to not take my eyes off him, was overwhelming. I couldn't even try to avert my gaze, my inability to ignore him was just as strong as it was the day I met him.

And just like that day, I needed to not fall into the

trap of his eyes, his essence, whatever it was that made Lord Quill so compelling.

Ash had said Lord Quill didn't have any magic, but I begged to differ.

His golden hair and sculpted, almost boyish face, possessed power, and it took everything within me to ignore the burning in my mating marks and tear my gaze away.

It's just his beauty. Nothing more.

"Hello," the woman said as she strode through the sitting room and into the bedroom, her pale blue robe swirling around her with each step. "I'm Zinnia, a healer."

"Welcome magister," Onyx said as he rose from his stool and stepped back, offering her the stool.

She sat and her gaze quickly slid over me before her kind eyes met mine. "Quill said you needed healing. May I?"

"I ah..."

All the tales said a fae with healing magic could know everything about a person with a single touch. That was why I knew I had to avoid Flint, the healer at the Black Tower, at all costs. One touch and he'd know I was a girl.

One touch now and would Zinnia know I was human?

"It's all right, Sage," Ash murmured, his warm breath fluttering against my cheek. "It won't hurt."

That wasn't what I was worried about.

"I-I really don't want to trouble you," I stammered.

It was a stupid excuse because Lord Quill had already troubled her by dragging her here, but it was the only thing I could think of.

"Can you remove the bracelet instead?" I lifted my arm and showed her the intricately wrought silver bracelet trapping me in the Garden. "It's keeping my spirit in the Garden. I'm sure I'll be fine once I've returned to my body."

Zinnia frowned. "It's not that simple. Injuries sustained in spirit form manifest on the physical body. They won't simply disappear when you return. And I'm a healer. I can't influence artifacts."

Crap.

I had to let her touch me.

My lieu time was only a couple of days and it would take longer than that for the rope burn on my wrists and the cut on my cheek to heal. And while the shirtsleeves of my guard uniform were too long, I couldn't guarantee they wouldn't rise up and someone wouldn't notice.

Lord Rider would know immediately who I was the second he saw my new wounds.

I swallowed at my rising panic determined to keep it down and prayed Zinnia wouldn't notice I was human. "All right."

The healer offered me a soft smile that I was sure

was supposed to make me feel better, then turned to the guys. "You should wait in the sitting room."

Lord Rider's expression darkened and he grunted before turning and storming out of the bedroom. Talon, Lord Quill, and Onyx followed, while Ash's grip tightened around me as if he didn't want to stop holding me.

I didn't want him to stop holding me, either.

But I also couldn't afford for him to learn I was a human. There was a slim chance I'd be able to convince Zinnia not to say anything, but that would only work if the guys weren't in the room.

On top of that, I had questions about these frustrating mating marks that I didn't want Ash to know. Just thinking about him hearing my questions made my cheeks heat with embarrassment.

I met his dark gaze. "I'll be fine."

"I know you will." He brushed his lips against my temple, sending desire surging through my veins then slipped off the bed and settled me against the headboard propped up by the pillows.

His shoulders squared as if it took effort for him to walk away, but he still strode from the room and shut the door without looking back.

I dragged my attention back to Zinnia, my pulse pounding.

I could do this.

I could convince her not to say anything.

Everything would work out and I'd wake in the Black Tower feeling great.

Except I couldn't feel great. I had to have a bruise on my cheek where Ambrose had punched me, and I needed to look — or at least act — like I'd run on the trail for hours.

"So ah..." I grabbed the edge of the blanket and started to pull it away.

But Zinnia placed a hand on mine. "That won't be necessary."

"Oh. Right. Of course."

She could heal me with just a touch. She didn't need to see my injuries.

Damn it. I was giving myself away and she hadn't even used her magic on me.

"Just relax."

"I ah... Could you—"

Zinnia took my hand in both of hers before I could ask if she would only partially heal me, and a soothing warmth rolled up my arm and seeped into my body. All the tension and strength in my muscles vanished, and I sagged back against the pillows even as my fear of discovery grew.

Please. Please. Don't let her realize...

My eyelids fluttered shut and I strained to open them. I had to keep watching. I needed to know the moment she discovered the truth.

But throbbing in the back of my skull melted away

— I hadn't realized how much it had hurt — and I floated on warmth and comfort. Then the warmth started to soothe the pain in my cheek where both Wells and Ambrose had hit me.

Shadows, that felt so good, so—

Panic surged through me.

Shit. I had to keep the bruise. The men in the Black Tower would ask questions if it were gone. I had to stop this.

CHAPTER 11
Sage

"STOP. PLEASE." I tried to draw my hand away from Zinnia but she held tight.

My panic squeezed my insides. I couldn't let her completely heal me. I had to keep some of my injuries even if my new ones could give me away. The new one would be easier to explain than the missing bruise on my cheek.

"No. That's enough." I wrenched my hand free and hugged it to my chest, afraid she'd reach for it and continue healing me. Her magic vanished in a flash, sending a chill rushing through me.

She jerked back and stiffened. "I haven't finished."

"That's ah... That's all right." I grabbed the blanket bunched at my waist and pulled it up to my neck. "I'm sure you've healed me enough. You should save your magic in case someone else needs you."

So far she hadn't mentioned anything about me being human and my cheek still hurt. I could only pray I'd have a bruise when I woke.

"I'm not sure there's anyone else who'll need me more," Zinnia replied.

"Well, I—" How did I convince her I needed the bruise on my face. I couldn't tell her I'd get in trouble if it was gone. Fae women were supposed to be precious and if Zinnia told Ash, he'd think I was being abused.

Shit shit shit.

He was going to think something was up if I stepped out of this bedroom and wasn't completely healed.

"Sage," Zinnia said, her tone gentle as if she were afraid to scare me. "I'm a master healer. I'm not beholden to anyone except the High Priestess. I've taken vows of secrecy. Unless you give me your permission, whatever happens, whatever you tell me, stays between us."

I met her milky blue gaze, desperate to figure out if I could trust her... desperate *to* trust her.

"I'm not supposed to be here," I said carefully.

"And you're supposed to have a bruise on your cheek," she replied, just as carefully.

"Yes."

"And you don't know that when I heal a spirit, I can't completely heal the physical body." She frowned.

"You've been raised in the human realm, haven't you? You're still there."

"Yes." There was no point in denying it. It was the most logical explanation for why I was clueless and had a bruise on my physical body.

"It's illegal for humans to have fae slaves." She leaned forward, her hands pressed against the mattress beside me. "I can send someone to get you. You don't have to stay where you are."

My pulse lurched. I couldn't let her send people to rescue me. "I can't leave. I—"

"You absolutely *can* leave," she shot back, her expression turning fierce. "They're hurting you and haven't taught you anything about your people."

"Please." I grabbed her hands. "I can't leave just yet. I'm—"

Come on. Think of something that will get her to back off.

"I'm protecting someone. A human child." Surely it would be illegal for the fae to kidnap a human child even in the name of protecting them. "I'm all he has and I can't leave until I know he's safe."

Zinnia's gaze captured mine and I met her head on. As much as I wanted to look away, bow to her greater status, I needed to stand firm. I had to protect Sawyer.

"You'll tell me the moment he's safe?"

"I will," I lied.

I was going to avoid Zinnia as much as possible.

Sure, she said she wouldn't tell anyone, but that didn't mean someone couldn't overhear our conversations.

My attention jumped to the bedroom door, still closed tight.

"You're also going to need to do something about your marks," Zinnia said. "They're fully awakened, and you need to ease the compulsion. I'm actually surprised you've held out this long."

I ducked my head, my cheeks heating.

"So you've tried to ease the compulsion, but your marks are still filled with power," Zinnia said, realizing right away from my blush that I'd been intimate with someone lately.

Who was I kidding? She probably knew from how Ash and I were cuddling when she'd walked in that it was Ash who'd help me relieve the pressure.

"You seem close with Ash," she added, confirming my fear that she knew who I was blushing over. "He's kind and protective. He'd make a good mate."

My blush deepened, rushing down my neck to swirl into the heat radiating from my marks. I didn't want a mate, but if it was Ash, maybe it would be all right. I'd felt safe with him from the moment we'd met and a part of me knew he wouldn't be angry when he learned I was human.

"That said... if you can't leave the human realm right now," Zinnia continued, "a mate would make things difficult."

"Yes," I agreed. "But what can I do?"

I still craved sex, needed it desperately, and I knew that feeling was going to follow me into the Gray.

I supposed I could have sex with a fae man who didn't have magic, but would I feel safe with him? Payne, one of my few possible friends in the Black Tower, had said a man without magic hadn't been bonded in a long time, but that didn't mean it couldn't happen.

And with the spell Wells had cast on me added with my current luck, I'd be bonded with the first man I had actual intercourse with whether he had magic or not.

"There's an unnatural magic exacerbating the power in your marks," Zinnia said. "I can't stop the magic. You'll need a spell magister to unravel it from your essence, but I can at least put your marks to sleep."

I opened my mouth to agree, but Zinnia held up a finger, stopping me.

"There are risks." Her expression turned grim. "I don't know when they would reawaken and I won't be able to reawaken them for you. There's also a possibility that your marks won't ever reawaken. Meaning you may never be able to find your mates and bond with them."

A strange sadness rippled through me at the thought, but I quickly shoved it away. I shouldn't regret something I wasn't supposed to have. I was human, and humans didn't create mate bonds with their spouses.

"Do it." I held out my hand. "Put my marks to sleep. I'm not ready for a mate."

Zinnia's expression turned worried.

"I don't know if I'll ever be ready," I added, hoping she wouldn't try to talk me out of it. "Not after what happened."

The worry turned to sadness and she took my hand. "I understand."

Once again, Zinnia's magic swept up my arm in a powerful rush, but instead of turning to a comforting warmth that radiated through my whole body, the heat chilled and headed to the spots curling around my neck and into my cleavage.

I shivered, the cold seeping into me, and tried to relax. It would be over soon, and I wouldn't have to worry about being mate bonded with anyone. I could just worry about keeping my secret and staying alive.

The desire radiating through me shuddered once... twice... before flaring stronger and making my eyes roll back. My breathing picked up and the ache in my core burned with need.

A moan bubbled in my throat, and I clenched my jaw, trying to keep it contained, but it slipped out, a gurgled, mangled sound of pleasure and pain.

Zinnia huffed and her grip on my hand tightened.

Her cool magic snapped to bone-freezing cold and pounded into me, no longer just focused on my marks.

Another moan escaped, this one all pain.

"Just breathe through it," Zinnia hissed through clenched teeth.

Shivers wracked my body, stealing my breath and making my teeth chatter. Red and pale blue light radiated from my mating marks, clashing against each other sending sparks flying around me and shooting pain through my chest.

"Just... a little... more." Zinnia squeezed her eyes closed and an icy wave of magic slammed into me.

The red and blue light exploded with a blinding brilliance, blacking out my vision and flooding me with frozen, screaming agony.

I clenched my jaw, refusing to scream — because that would make the guys rush into the room — and collapsed back against the pillows propping me up in the bed.

The cold slowly bled away and the darkness in my vision thinned and vanished. Exhaustion flooded my veins and the room seemed dimmer than before.

Everything was dimmer... and colder.

I glanced at my cleavage. The light was gone, and the mating marks were plain, magicless red spots on my skin. Except...

Was that one green?

And there! There was another one that looked green.

Why weren't they all red like they'd been before? Was that part of the spell?

Except Zinnia stared at my neck in shock, and the panic I was struggling to keep at bay surged.

"It's all right," Zinnia said, her expression snapping to what was supposed to be a comforting neutral as if I hadn't just seen her surprise. "When your marks change from your hair color to your eye color it means you've created a mate bond. But—"

"I've created a what!" I squeaked.

I couldn't be bonded with someone. I was human. I couldn't make bonds.

Who the hell was I bonded to?

"But," Zinnia said more firmly, "it just might be a side effect of putting your marks back to sleep." Her expression softened. "It could also mean the Goddess has blessed you with your first mate but knows you aren't ready yet. I can't sense magic in any of your marks, even the green ones, so the connection—"

I opened my mouth to deny that possibility. There was no connection. There'd never be a connection.

Oh, Great Father! What if there *was* a connection?

"If there *is* a connection," Zinnia said, "it's still asleep."

"So that means...?"

"Whoever your first mate is... And I'm not saying

you actually have one. He won't be aware that the Goddess has bonded your souls together," Zinnia said. "That will only happen once the magic in your marks reawakens."

Oh, Father. Please don't let my marks ever reawaken.

"I'm hoping this is a good sign," Zinnia added. "It means in the future, when you're safe, you'll be able to find your mates and live a happy life."

"Yeah," I mumbled back, trying my best to feign happiness at the thought.

Except, from Zinnia's expression, I'd failed miserably.

"The Goddess wouldn't bond you with someone you didn't trust. She only makes bonds when the spark of true love can blossom."

Except the Goddess hadn't stopped Wells from forming a mating bond with me, and I wasn't sure I trusted the fae's Goddess.

I wasn't sure I trusted anyone at the moment.

"Now," Zinnia said, her tone still gentle, but definitely back to business. "You might feel strange and still desire a physical release for a while. You've been accustomed to the warmth and heightened arousal from the marks, but soon you'll feel like you did before your marks awakened."

As she spoke a shiver of heated desire slid down to my core, reminding me that despite my lifeless mating marks, I was still somewhat aroused.

"How long until it goes away?"

"I don't know," she replied. "The number of recorded cases of someone putting their marks back to sleep can be counted on one hand... and that includes you. It could be hours or days. If it's longer than a few months you should see me again."

"A few months?" I could still have heightened arousal for a few months?

"Your body needs time to adjust. You might also experience flare-ups. But unless your marks are radiating light you won't be able to create a bond."

Or *another* bond.

I closed my eyes. Trying to focus on how the situation was good.

I could sleep with whoever I wanted and I wouldn't trap an unwitting fae man into mate bonding with me.

Except it felt like something essential had been ripped out of me. Even terrified that I already had a mate, a small part of me wept that he might never acknowledge me.

That I'd be alone. Forever.

But that was just because I'd gotten used to the marks. Nothing more.

Maybe this means I'll stop waking in the Garden every time I go to sleep?

A part of me was thrilled at the prospect. I wouldn't have to worry about men attacking me or trying to avoid Lord Rider and the others. I could focus on keeping my identity in the Black Tower a secret and give my brother as much time as possible to get away.

But another part of me ached at the thought. I wouldn't be able to meet with Ash again, wouldn't feel the comfort of being protected in his arms, or the pure bliss that swept through me every time he made me come.

A sharp knock on the door jolted me from my thoughts and I scrambled to pull the blanket up to my neck to cover my mating marks. The door creaked open, but not wide enough for me to see who was on the other side.

Zinnia straightened, her pale blue robe rustling softly, and met my gaze. I could see the question in her eyes: did I want whoever it was to come in?

I nodded. I couldn't avoid the guys forever, and I didn't want to be excluded from the investigation. I needed to know just how dangerous my situation was.

"We're finished here," she said. "You may come in."

The door swung open fully and Lord Quill stepped into the room.

Something zinged through me. It was the same feeling I got every time we touched, except now we were currently a room apart.

Was he my newly bonded mate?

"Thank you, Zinnia," Lord Quill said, before turning his attention to me. "The High Priestess has learned about the attack. She's summoned everyone involved."

"Everyone?" I'd hoped by telling Onyx everything, I wouldn't have to face anyone else, especially not someone as powerful as the High Priestess, the woman who ruled all the fae.

"Everyone," Lord Quill confirmed, his expression grim.

CHAPTER 12

Sage

DREAD SETTLED in my gut at the thought of meeting the High Priestess. Surely she'd see right through me and know right away I was really a human.

Zinnia turned to Lord Quill. "Give us a moment."

With a nod, he stepped back out of the bedroom and closed the door with a soft click.

"Can you change your spirit form clothes?" she asked as soon as the door shut. "Your current ones are wet, and you covered up quite quickly when Quill entered. Clearly, you don't want them to see your marks."

I opened my mouth to respond but nothing came out. A part of me was shocked Zinnia would suggest I continue covering my marks. It didn't make sense for the fae to encourage me.

But she'd taken my discomfort about some of my

marks changing color seriously. I didn't have to explain to her that I didn't want to deal with the questions and looks I'd receive once the other fae saw me... once Lords Quill, Rider, Talon, and Ash saw me.

Oh, Father. Would Ash be upset that my marks might have selected a mate or would he be hopeful?

I wasn't sure if either was good.

And yet, something in my heart, something small and aching and lonely, wanted him to be mine.

I squeezed my eyes shut, shoving that feeling as deep down as possible.

I couldn't afford to want things.

I couldn't afford to have hope.

All I could do was survive.

"I understand if you're not ready for the questions," Zinnia said, taking my hesitation for the uncertainty that it was. "Only our elders remember the last time a woman had her marks put to sleep, and I doubt you'd meet any of them here. Even the three elders on the Elder Council barely spend time in the throne room."

My stomach clenched. "Right. The throne room."

Was that where I was meeting the High Priestess?

My pulse picked up. Maybe it would be a private audience. Maybe I wouldn't be forced into such a public setting, because without a doubt if the High Priestess was in her throne room, the fae nobility would be there as well.

"Sage," Zinnia said, resting a hand on my blanket-covered thigh. "It'll be all right. Just answer the High Priestess's questions as honestly as you can and let those men out there waiting for you and the Order's knights take care of the rest."

I met her milky blue gaze. The understanding in her eyes made my throat tighten. She thought I was a slave in the human realm. She knew I knew next to nothing about being a fae woman, and it was clear she wanted to help.

She sat back with a soft smile. "Now, let's change your clothes."

"How do I do that?"

"All you need to do is imagine yourself wearing what you want to wear."

"Just like that?" It seemed far too simple.

"Just like that," she replied.

I closed my eyes, ready to imagine myself in something that covered me from neck to ankle. The fashion I was used to had high necklines, long sleeves, and hems that brushed the ground... or at least the clothes I used to wear when my mother was alive. Once I'd become my stepfather's maid, my hem rose to just above my ankles, so I wouldn't trip, and the neckline loosened just a bit.

Except that was human fashion and human women weren't supposed to draw attention to themselves or their sexuality.

Here in the Garden, my dress barely covered the

important bits, and of the three other fae women I'd seen, two of them had worn dresses just as revealing as mine.

Only Zinnia wore something that completely covered her, the collar of her robe high enough that I couldn't even catch a glimpse of her mating marks.

I concentrated on turning my lacey gauzy dress into a thick robe like Zinnia's. I imagined it green instead of blue and focused on how the collar would stand up, brushing the edge of my jaw and covering all of my spots.

But it didn't feel as if anything was happening.

I didn't get the sense there was more fabric around my body, that the gauzy lacy dress I always materialized in was changing into a thick robe.

All I really felt was exhausted, sore, turned on — still! — and damp.

I opened my eyes and peeled back the blanket.

Yep, still in the red dress.

A sharp knock on the door made me jump. "We shouldn't keep the High Priestess waiting," Lord Quill called out.

I squeezed my eyes shut and tried again, concentrating on how the soft, heavy fabric of the robe would feel. I'd be warm and dry and covered.

Please, Great Father, let me be covered.

But nothing happened.

With a huff, I opened my eyes.

"For all we know the artifact keeping your spirit here is keeping you from changing your clothes," Zinnia said. "Let's keep you bundled in the blanket so you don't catch a chill. Healer's orders."

She helped me to my feet, making sure I had a good grip on the blanket ensuring it covered my marks and so I wouldn't trip, before she hurried me out of the bedroom into a sitting room.

Plush furniture was situated in front of a crackling fire in a fieldstone fireplace, but I was too nervous about meeting the High Priestess and keeping my marks hidden to fully take in the rest of the details of the room.

All four of the men who'd rescued me, along with Onyx, stood in the room and stared at me. Lord Quill's eyes, along with Onyx's, were wide with surprise as if they didn't expect me to still look like a drowned cat. Talon's expression remained serious, not revealing any reaction to my appearance, while Lord Rider's glare darkened, making me feel like I'd done something to seriously displease him.

My gaze slid to Ash. I'd been trying not to look at him, afraid of his reaction now that we'd had a moment apart. He'd made me feel amazing and protected, but I now knew his name and knew why he'd been keeping his identity from me.

While we'd been together in the bedroom, every-thing had been perfect, our own little realm away from everything else. But in the brighter sitting room, things could be different.

I ached at the thought. I understood why he hadn't wanted me to see him, but I didn't care about his appearance. He gave me something I'd never had before, something I'd never thought I would ever have: feeling safe in a man's arms.

But he stood at the back of the room by the door as if desperate to leave, his head tilted forward so his jaw-length hair veiled the right side of his face and partially obscured his scars.

His dark gaze slid up to meet mine, his eyes filled with a sad wariness that made my heart hurt.

Did he think I'd reject him now that my marks no longer made me desperate?

I took a step toward him, ready to tell him I'd never reject him. He was the only man I felt safe with. He was the only person in the Garden I trusted.

But Lord Rider jerked forward from his spot by the fire, his posture radiating danger. "Why isn't she healed?"

I shrunk back from him, unable to resist the compulsion, and all the men, including Rider, froze.

"There's an unnatural magic affecting her." Zinnia shifted forward and partially shielded me from Rider. "I've used my magic to help mitigate the effects, but until it's gone I can't properly heal her. And," she added before Rider could say anything else, "the magic affecting her or the artifact that is keeping her here is preventing her from changing her spirit form clothes."

"Fuck," Rider growled.

Quill glared at him. "It is what it is. Let's go. We've already kept Her Brilliance waiting."

CHAPTER 13

Sage

AFTER WALKING THROUGH THE TWISTING, dimly lit passages of the magical grove, we arrived at a large, imposing archway cut into the trunk of the massive tree-castle structure that towered over the Garden.

Above, wide branches reached around and through stone structures, acting like supports or open-air hallways, and lights glimmered from windows, illuminating intricately carved windowsills and balconies.

Ahead of me, the archway opened to a wide hall. It was the now familiar, yet still incredible half-stone, half-wood impossible blend. The walls were a mix of the wood and stone, and the floor was marble, polished to a gleam. Intricate chandeliers hung from the ceiling filled with magical fae light — noticeable because the lights didn't flicker like a flame would.

Rider strode forward, leading the way. Lord Quill

followed, one step behind his Lord Commander, and Onyx fell into step beside Quill, while Zinnia pressed a hand against my back and urged me forward, walking with me.

Hopefully she'd stay by my side for the whole encounter. I might have been a nobleman's daughter, but I was human. I knew how to behave before the King of Erellod and his nobles in the human realm, but I had no idea how to behave in front of the High Priestess.

And Talon's order that very first night I met him in the bathing room under the Black Tower, that I don't look at my feet even when presented to the High Priestess, only applied if I was a Guardsman.

Which, at the moment, I wasn't.

I tightened my grip on the blanket wrapped around my shoulders, my knuckles turning white with the strain, and resisted the urge to look over my shoulder and seek comfort from Ash.

I wasn't sure he'd offer it. Our walk to the throne room felt more like an official procession with Talon and Ash as the rearguard, and if that were the case, he probably wouldn't react to me even if he wanted to.

I didn't know if the guys were doing it on purpose, but if I was smart, I'd use our arrangement to appear strong and not like I was a prisoner being marched to the dungeon — which was the other possible interpretation for our positions.

With my death grip on my blanket, I squared my shoulders. I didn't want to be strong. I was scared and sore and exhausted. But I didn't want anyone else thinking I was an easy target. I didn't want to draw attention to myself, but I also didn't want to invite an attack by letting people know how upset I was.

Wells might be dead, but some of the men got away. Maybe if I acted like Ember, the woman who'd walked into the courtyard and commanded the attention of every man there, my attackers would give up on their plans to bond with me.

The thought made my insides squirm. It went against everything I'd been taught. Even spending a rotation as a man couldn't eliminate the fear of reprisal for being a woman who wasn't afraid.

But there weren't any other options.

The hall ended at two heavy doors intricately carved with vines and blooming flowers. Two guards stood at attention, their armor gleaming in the magical light, their fabric colors matching what Onyx wore, indicating these men were Knights of the Order of the Sacred Grove.

As we drew near, the guards pushed open the doors, revealing a massive chamber beyond. The throne room.

It was enormous. I couldn't believe how large and majestic it was. I could barely make out the woman on the throne at the other end of the room, and no one in the crowd standing before the throne's high dais. The sides of the room were wreathed in shadows, and a mix of tree trunks and marble pillars, standing in two even lines and creating a wide central aisle toward the throne, held up a ceiling that soared high above us.

Just like the hall, the throne room continued the blending of wood and stone walls and gleaming marble floor. Large, arched windows lined the walls, their stained glass depicting scenes of fae women being pleasured by multiple mates, and flowering vines framed each window, their blooms pulsing with that soft, magical light.

Rider paused briefly in the doorway as if to make a statement about our arrival — but more likely to let me close my gaping mouth before reaching the High Priestess. Then he continued his steady, confident stride forward.

The front of the room was just as awe-inspiring as the rest. It ended with a recessed area as wide across as the center aisle, and in the recess stood a high dais with a massive throne sitting on it and a spectacular, large stained glass window behind it. The window was a starburst with streaking gold, orange, and red glass, and it gleamed with a brilliant light as if the sun shone through the window even though it was night.

Just below the window, the focus of that light, was the High Priestess's throne. It, too, was shaped like a starburst, with golden strips of various lengths and sizes protruding from behind it. More of the flowering vines that I'd seen everywhere in the sacred grove, entwined around it, trailing around its base and curling over its arms and back.

Sitting on the throne and somehow not dwarfed by the large structure, was the most beautiful — and powerful — woman I'd ever seen.

Her eyes were so pale I couldn't tell what color they were and her hair cascaded down in shimmering golden waves, catching the light with every slight movement. She wore a shimmering white gown, the bodice cut wider and lower than mine, her full modesty only maintained by the radiant white mating marks glowing so brightly around her neck and trailing into her cleavage it was difficult to see her pale flesh.

Beside the throne stood three large, powerful fae men, two on the right, one on the left. One of the men on the right was dressed in a green and gold tunic, while the other two wore variations of the armor the knights at the door had worn.

All three had bare arms, exposing the radiant white bands ringing their biceps, the proof that they were the High Priestess's mates.

At the foot of the dozen stairs that led up to the dais, stood four knights holding polearms. I noticed two more knights standing at doors on either side of the recess's edges, and when I glanced beside me, I noticed another knight standing in the shadows near the wall.

The crowd that had stood before the throne at the bottom of the stairs parted as we approached. There were dozens of them, mostly men, but I did notice four women, mainly because the men had moved to ensure the women had unobscured views of me. They all stared with hungry and judging gazes, and whispers rippled through the crowd.

The urge to hide squeezed my insides. I felt like prey.

Who was I kidding?

I *was* prey.

They all wore fine clothes. The women and some of the men wore flashy jewelry around their necks and wrists, in their ears, and woven into their hair.

This was the fae nobility. Even if I hadn't looked like I'd been beaten and drowned, I wouldn't have belonged, and they knew it.

And one, perhaps more, of these men could have been involved in attacking me.

CHAPTER 14
Sage

LORD RIDER STOPPED ten feet from the base of the stairs and stepped to the side, ruining any hope I had that I could hide from the High Priestess's gaze behind his broad back. Lord Quill stepped to the other side, straightening as well, and Onyx stepped ahead of Lord Rider.

Onyx dropped to one knee and bowed his head, while Lord Rider, Quill, Talon, and Ash jerked straight, each stomped their right foot, and stood at attention.

Zinnia sank gracefully to her knees and bowed her head, and I half sagged, half dropped to the hard marble floor with a thud, my leg muscles screaming at the movement, reminding me that I'd run for hours and told Zinnia not to completely heal me.

Through my lashes, I watched the High Priestess stare at me, her impossibly pale gaze intense.

Could she tell I was human?

The moment stretched on and my pulse thumped faster and faster. No one said anything. Even the crowd around us remained silent.

She knew.

She had to know.

Even though humans didn't have the magic to send their spirits anywhere and only fae could be in the Garden, she *knew* I was an anomaly, an intruder.

She was going to command her knights to take me away and my body was going to stay sleeping in the Gray without my soul until I withered and died.

Her gaze slid away, moving over the rest of our group, her expression never changing, betraying nothing.

"I've heard rumors," the High Priestess said, her voice ringing proud and strong in the massive throne room, "that the silence of the sacred pool has been disturbed."

Her gaze slid to Onyx and her eyes narrowed, the only indication that she felt something. And that *feeling* wasn't good.

"Tell me, Sir Onyx. How are you involved in the incident?"

"Your Brilliance," Onyx replied, his head still bowed. "The nature of the situation is... delicate. Captain Talon approached me to assist in handling the matter."

The High Priestess's expression returned to firm neutrality. "What could be so delicate that Captain Talon of the Black Guard would seek out a knight captain of the Order on his day off?"

Onyx tilted his head toward the crowd, and I realized he was trying to get the High Priestess to dismiss the onlookers without asking her to do so.

Father, that would be wonderful. I was determined to ignore them, but I could feel them staring at me. It made my insides squirm. And while I couldn't make out their words, I had no doubt their whispers were all about me.

But after a beat that was too short — making me feel like he'd given up too easily on his request — but also too long not to feel awkward, he straightened his head, his eyes still downcast. "Your Brilliance, a group of men attacked Sage, the new arrival."

A collective gasp rippled through the crowd, followed by a swell of shocked murmurs.

I cringed, wishing I could melt into the floor, and knowing I couldn't let all the men around me see my fear.

I could only pray they now saw me as damaged goods and wouldn't want to pursue me.

But I got the impression being *damaged* meant they'd think I was easier to obtain. I could see it now. These men thought because Wells and Crane had treated me badly a little bit of fake kindness would win me over.

But I already knew what happened with fake kindness.

I ended up too sore to stand and puking in the dirt.

A hint of something gleamed in the High Priestess's eyes so fast I wasn't sure I saw it. Her expression certainly didn't change. She didn't even shift positions on her throne.

And yet everything within me said she was enjoying herself, enjoying seeing me on my knees even though she didn't know me, and enjoying the attention.

"I see," she said. "And Lord Commander Rider? How exactly did you and your captains become involved in this situation."

"Your Brilliance," Lord Rider said, his voice deep and powerful. "Captain Ash noticed the abduction and gathered me, Captain Talon, and Captain Quill to mount a rescue."

My pulse stuttered and I fought to not look at Ash. *He* was another captain in the Black Guard? He couldn't be. I trusted him.

But in my heart, I knew the High Priestess's words had to be true. He was too familiar with Lord Rider, Talon, and Lord Quill not to be involved in the Black Guard somehow.

Sure they could have been close friends, perhaps

even lovers, but they worked too well together for just that. They were clearly a team. Given the fae's lifespan, they'd probably spent years working together.

Of course, if Ash was a captain in the Black Guard, did that mean if Lord Rider commanded, would he abandon me like Lord Quill and Talon did?

The moment I thought that, though, I knew it was ridiculous.

Something in my soul assured me I was safe with Ash, that no matter what his position in the Black Guard and fae hierarchy, he'd always put me first.

"We were able to stop whatever Wells and his co-conspirators were planning," Rider said, "but some of them managed to escape."

The High Priestess's firm, emotionless expression shattered and fury blazed in her eyes.

I flinched, every muscle contracting trying to keep me in my bowed position while also making me small, as small as humanly possible. Power radiated from her and light flared from her marks and blazed in her eyes.

She could crush me with a thought. One flick of her fingers and her knights would skewer me. Hell, one flick of her fingers and the power roaring around her would kill me.

And it felt like all of her fury was directed at me.

Somehow I was responsible for what had happened in the sacred pool and I was going to pay.

The courtiers around us gasped at the High Priestess's sudden rage and a flurry of whispers swept through the crowd.

"Desecration of the sacred pool will not be tolerated," she hissed, her voice too soft but still, impossibly, echoing in the vast throne room. "Every last man involved will be hunted down and punished for this outrage."

Her gaze snapped to me, and I flinched again.

"You may raise your head, child," she purred, her change of tone doing little to reassure me. "You must be shaken and frightened after such an ordeal."

Another flurry of whispers rushed through the crowd as I raised my head and met the High Priestess's unnerving, colorless gaze.

That gleam flashed again in the High Priestess's eyes, just as quickly as before, but I was certain now that I'd seen it.

"You're safe now," she assured me, her expression softening. But the emotions didn't reach her gaze. "My knights will take care of everything now."

CHAPTER 15
Sage

"FIRST THOUGH," the High Priestess said as if my safety was second in consideration to whatever she was going to say next. "Tell me of your family. Are any of them here in the Garden?"

My pulse picked up and sweat slicked my palms as I clutched the blanket.

This was a trap. It had to be.

The whispers of the courtiers grew louder, and their gazes burned into me from all sides, hungry and expectant.

Except I had no idea what to say. I didn't want to lie. Everything within me screamed that she'd be able to sense an outright lie.

"Why...?" The High Priestess continued, her previous soft expression — or as soft as I'd seen so far — sliding back to her serious, firm mask. "Why haven't you been fully healed and properly attired? Why didn't you pay me the appropriate respect when you first entered the Garden? Everyone, including my court, has been abuzz with talk of you for days."

My stomach twisted tighter. I didn't know which was worse: her sudden dangerous rage, or this cool, feigned compassion. In fact, everything about her felt like an act.

Everything except her power.

The magical strength and command radiating from her was real, and she had everyone in the room exactly where she wanted them.

"Y-Your ah..." What had Onyx and Lord Rider called her? "Your B-Brilliance..." I stammered, my soft words devoured by the cavernous throne room.

"Speak up, child," the High Priestess said in a sing-song, making me feel even more like her plaything.

More whispers skittered through the crowd, and a shiver rushed down my spine at the hungry expressions from the men closest to me.

This was why I'd avoided the courtyard. I didn't want anyone looking at me like that.

Well... I wanted my Fantasy Man, Ash, to look at me like that.

And the part I was damn well going to ignore wanted Lords Rider, Quill, and Talon to look at me like that as well.

Be strong, I mentally hissed at myself.

Except what could I say? I didn't want to confess I needed to keep my injuries or that I couldn't change my spirit clothes like everyone could. And I hadn't known I was supposed to introduce myself to the High Priestess when I first arrived. I hadn't known anything.

Hell, I still didn't know anything.

"I-I apologize, Your Brilliance," I forced out, my stutter echoing around the chamber and ringing in my ears. Father, why couldn't I speak normally in front of the dangerous, powerful woman? "I didn't mean any disrespect. I—"

"Your Brilliance," Zinnia said from her kneeling position beside me, her head still bowed in respect. "If I may speak?"

The High Priestess's clear gaze leveled on Zinnia. "Speak."

Zinnia raised her head. "Lady Sage suffered a blow to the head during the attack, and her memories are muddled. Combined with the shock of the assault, it's unclear when her full faculties will return."

I resisted the urge to stare at Zinnia or let my mouth fall open in shock. The woman was lying to the High Priestess, the highest power in the fae realm, to protect me.

Sure, she might pity me because she thought I was a slave in the human realm, but she was still risking everything.

Something dark flickered in the High Priestess's

gaze, once again there and gone in a flash, but her expression didn't change.

"That's a very troubling condition," the High Priestess replied.

"It is," Zinnia agreed. "Head injuries are compli-cated and working on Sage's has taken most of my power."

The High Priestess raised a sculpted, delicate eyebrow. "Surely she'd have her memories to show for all your hard work."

"Sadly the best anyone can do, is to stabilize the injury," Zinnia replied.

"You must continue to monitor her condition." The High Priestess slid her gaze back to me and her eyes narrowed. "Some of the assailants who desecrated the sacred pool are still at large."

A hint of her rage from before burned through her mask, and my mouth went dry.

She was back to blaming me.

And from the murmurs coming from the courtiers, they'd noticed it, too.

"While my knights conduct the investigation, you'll need protection," she said, her tone turning to that unsettling purr again. "Since you don't know of your family and no one has stepped forward and claimed you as their daughter—"

"Your Brilliance," Lord Rider said, brazenly interrupting her. "I volunteer myself and my captains to protect Lady Sage whenever she's in the Garden."

More murmurs rushed through the crowd, this time loud enough for me — and Lord Rider from his scowl — to hear.

"Rider volunteering?"

"—has chosen to mate."

"Does this mean—?"

"—so disrespectful—"

"It has to be his wolf."

I stared at Rider's wide, straight back as he rumbled a low, dangerous growl.

Just like everyone else, I couldn't believe he'd volunteered to protect me. Him and the other guys saving me from Wells and Crane could be written off as a one-time thing, something their honorable natures compelled them to do. But being willing to meet me every night and stay with me for as long as I was in the Garden was something completely different.

I just didn't know what it meant. It went against everything I'd learned about them. Before being attacked, Lord Rider had only said a few words to me in the Garden before fleeing. Talon had said even fewer words and had been mean about it because he couldn't afford to be mate bonded and have his mate discover that a shadow entity was trapped within his body.

The only one who'd been nice to me was Lord

Quill and, just like with Talon, we'd barely exchanged words.

As for Ash, I caught him tensing when Rider volunteered him which made my throat tighten with disappointment.

I wanted him to *want* to protect me.

Hell, I ridiculously wanted all of them to protect me.

But Ash also hadn't met me every night I'd been in the Garden.

I didn't know what he did for the Black Guard — I had yet to meet him in the Black Tower — but not meeting me every night might mean his job kept him busier than even the others' jobs.

And really! The more time I spent with them in the Garden, the more likely it would be they'd figure out my secret.

I didn't want to be constantly near them all the time...

Even if I *did* want to be constantly near them all the time.

The High Priestess tsked, jerking me from my thoughts.

"Lord Commander," she said as she dismissed him with a lazy flick of her fingers. "Your duties and your captains' duties to the Black Guard require all of your attention. The protection of the Gray and the Gates of the Realms against the shadows is paramount."

That gleam flashed in her eyes again.

"We must assign a guard who can be available at all times." Her lips curled back in a smile that I was sure was supposed to be kind but wasn't. "Sir West."

Something heavy thumped from far behind me, the sound echoing in the chamber, and I turned to see a massive figure in a knight's uniform emerging from the shadows against the wall near the back of the throne room.

He strode to the center aisle and marched confidently toward the throne, his footsteps thundering in the suddenly quiet chamber.

He was enormous, a monster. He was taller and broader than even Rider, and his long, coppery hair was tied back in a severe ponytail, accentuating his square, blocky face, and his grim expression.

But it wasn't just his size that stunned me. He was the first fae I'd seen who wasn't shockingly beautiful. He was barely handsome by fae standards.

The only thing stunning about him were his brilliant sapphire eyes.

He strode past me without even looking at me, then past Lord Rider and Talon, and dropped to one knee beside Onyx and bowed his head.

"Your Brilliance," he rumbled.

I stared at him and shivered, fighting the terror rising within me.

He'd moved with a predatory grace like Lord Rider,

and I couldn't help wondering if he was an animal shifter, too. Regardless, it didn't matter if he could turn into an animal, or even if he could wield the two massive swords hanging from each hip — which I was certain he could — Sir West could kill me. He probably wouldn't even need his hands. Just a finger would probably be powerful enough.

On top of that he looked young — not that it was easy to tell a fae's age. But somehow I just knew he was unmated and couldn't help worrying if he'd been involved in my attack.

I didn't recognize him, but that didn't mean Wells and Crane hadn't planned to add more men to my pack of unwanted mates after the initial forced bonding ceremony.

Even if West hadn't been involved. If he decided he wanted me to satisfy his needs, I wouldn't be able to resist him.

Wells had proven not all fae men respected and treated women with kindness, and from Sir West's grimace, I feared he was the same.

And this was the man the High Priestess wanted to stay with me every time I entered the Garden.

CHAPTER 16

Sage

THE HIGH PRIESTESS stood and motioned for Sir West to approach her on the dais.

He rose and climbed the dozen steps to momentarily tower above the High Priestess on her throne before kneeling at her feet.

"Sir West." She placed a hand on his head and a white light burst to life where she touched him. "You're a knight of rising esteem. I command you to escort and protect the Lady Sage in the Garden until she has bound all her mates to her soul."

A gasp rippled through the courtiers and my pulse lurched.

Until I bound all my mates? But that meant—

The High Priestess wasn't just ordering Sir West to protect me until all of my attackers were apprehended.

She was ordering him to protect me until I was fully mated.

Except Zinnia had put my mating marks to sleep, marks that she said might never wake up, and I was human. Human! I didn't actually *have* mating marks. I wasn't ever going to be mated to anyone!

Really!

And if I never figured out how to stop waking in the Garden, Sir West would be at my side forever.

The light radiating from the High Priestess's hand flared blindingly bright. Black spots danced in my vision, and something hot, like a blast of fire, snapped in my chest.

I gasped, my hand flying to my heart.

What the—?

Had my mating marks reawakened?

Please no.

"I've spirit linked you with Lady Sage," the High Priestess announced, sending more whispers and gasps rushing through the crowd. "You'll know whenever she's in the Garden and exactly where she is."

Cold flashed through me, a shocking contrast to the heat from the spirit link.

This couldn't be happening.

How could I hide who I was with this monster constantly at my side?

Was I even safe with him?

The High Priestess flicked her fingers and a short

servant scurried forward and dropped to his knees at the foot of the stairs.

"Arrange a shared room for the lady and her knight," the High Priestess said, "as well as a spirit anchor."

Father, I didn't like the sound of that. Was a spirit anchor like the horrible bracelet currently keeping me trapped in the Garden?

And a shared room!

I didn't know how *shared* the room would be, but the idea terrified me more than just wandering around the Garden with Sir West constantly at my side.

With a room, Sir West could do anything he wanted to me and no one would be there to stop him.

The High Priestess sank back onto her throne. "Your ward, Sir West."

The monster stood, towering over me on the dais, and turned to face me, his expression just as grim as before, possibly even grimmer.

I shrank back, unable to stop myself from curling inward, trying to get as small as possible. It didn't matter that I wasn't supposed to look like prey in front of the High Priestess's court. Everything within me screamed Sir West was dangerous.

"Stand, child," the High Priestess snapped, her firm mask cracking.

The show was done and she wanted to get rid of me.

I staggered to my feet, clutching my blanket as if that would protect me against the monster I'd just been spirit linked to.

The High Priestess's lips curled into a sharp smile. "Please attend my court while we resolve your safety, Lady Sage. You have a bright spark and should make advantageous matches among my nobility."

I bobbed my head, knowing I wouldn't be able to raise my voice beyond a whisper.

I wanted to be strong— *needed* to be strong, but every time I steadied myself something else happened and it had all become too much before I'd even entered the Garden that night.

"Has your spark awakened? Do you know your magic?" The sharpness in her smile flashed in her eyes. Except I couldn't tell if she was playing with me because she knew I was human, or if she were just a cat and liked to play with her food before lunging in for the kill.

My gaze darted at the crowd around me. The hungry stares had intensified and their silence crushed me as they waited for my answer.

No, she wasn't a cat. She was a puppet spider. She toyed with her food for entertainment and to draw the attention of more prey before making the kill.

"Your Brilliance," Lord Quill said.

"Yes, *Captain* Quill," she replied with a strange emphasis on *captain.*

"With your permission, I'll escort Lady Sage to her chambers."

The High Priestess leveled her colorless stare at Lord Quill.

My pulse pounded and I prayed she'd say yes. I wasn't sure I trusted Lord Quill, but I certainly *didn't* trust Sir West.

"To her chambers tonight," she said, the message clear: don't get distracted and forget your duty to the Black Guard.

She waved her hand dismissively, and Sir West took that as his cue to stomp down the stairs and stop in front of me. I had to strain my neck to look up at him.

Father, he was big.

I was a child compared to him.

"My lady." Sir West gestured to the servant who stood impatiently at the edge of the stairs.

"I'll be along shortly," Zinnia whispered, squeezing my arm gently.

Right. Even if Lord Quill had to leave, Zinnia had been ordered to monitor my supposed amnesia. Still—

I glanced back at Ash. Now, more than ever, I wanted him with me.

Please.

But his gaze never jumped to mine, and I was afraid to speak up and ask for what I wanted. I didn't want to be rejected in front of all the hungry men and judging women, let alone the ruler of the fae people.

Please.

I didn't want to be trapped with that dour monster.

"You're dismissed, Lady Sage," the High Priestess snapped, making me flinch.

Pull yourself together!

Lord Quill offered me his arm and I took it to help steady myself. That zing I always felt when we touched snapped through me, stealing my breath, and my gaze locked with his for a heart-stalling moment. He was so beautiful, so kind... so obedient to Lord Rider.

"I'll stay on top of the investigation," Rider said, his voice low, as I wrenched my attention away from Lord Quill. "Talon, wait for the magister who can get that bracelet off her."

"I'll send a servant to let you know what room she's in," Quill added, before leading me toward the impatient servant who stood at the door waiting to leave the throne room.

Sir West fell into step behind us, but there was no way I could pretend he wasn't there. His dark intensity rolled off him in palpable waves, reminding me that my spirit was linked to his for as long as I remained unmated.

CHAPTER 17
Talon

SAGE DISAPPEARED through the door at the edge of the recess, her small, battered form dwarfed by West's massive frame. My shadow writhed beneath my skin, desperate to protect her from the knight, but I forced it to stay contained. At least Quill was with her.

For some reason, the High Priestess hadn't forbidden him from escorting Sage, which was surprising given her earlier dismissal of our offer to protect her.

Perhaps she sensed how fragile Sage was after the attack and didn't want to completely isolate her. Or perhaps she had other motives. With Her Brilliance, there were always other motives.

My shadow squeezed tighter within me, its worry and anger matching my own. The pressure was almost unbearable, but I couldn't risk letting even a whisper of its presence show. The courtiers would notice immediately, and the High Priestess would demand my arrest for not being able to control my magic.

I turned to leave with Rider, Ash, Onyx, and Zinnia, eager to get away from the throne room and the too-intense stares.

"A word, Captain Talon." The High Priestess's voice froze me in place.

She stood from her throne and strode toward the stairs at the edge of the dais. Her three mates fell into step behind her as she descended to the marble floor and glided to the door on the opposite side of the recess from where Sage had exited.

My stomach clenched. I didn't want a private audience with the High Priestess. I wanted to go to the entrance to the Sacred Grove and wait for the magister that was going to release Sage from the artifact binding her soul to the Garden.

I glanced at Rider, but his silver gaze remained hard. His wolf had been unstable before Sage had been attacked, and even if he wasn't going to mate her, his primal drive to protect all females had to be driving him crazy.

"I'll meet you at the grove's entrance," he growled, indicating with that simple sentence that he'd take care of the magister if the High Priestess decided to keep me.

I suppressed a shudder and followed the High Priestess and her mates through the door. Her Brilliance had already bonded to all her mates, and she wasn't inclined to invite other men to her bed, but that didn't mean she couldn't change her mind. Summoning me to entertain her and her mates could be a way to punish me for showing an interest in another woman.

She hadn't cared before who I'd slept with, but I'd also spent decades avoiding the High Priestess's court. With my looks, I was a highly sought-after prize, and Her Brilliance liked her prizes. My interest in Sage now could make her feel she was losing me even if she never had me to begin with.

The hall behind the throne room was just as impressive as the hall leading up to the throne room. The High Priestess and her mates stepped through the first door on the right into her private receiving room, and I forced myself to follow them inside.

My shadow writhed within me, tiny jerky movements around the core of my being, its anxiety and anger making my stomach churn. I didn't know what Her Brilliance wanted, but I doubted it was about Sage's well-being.

The private receiving room was a miniature version of the throne room, complete with a smaller version of her throne and the stained glass window behind it. Unlike the throne room, this throne didn't sit on a dais, but there still weren't other chairs or places to sit in the room.

The High Priestess took her seat and her three mates — the Lord Commander of the Order of the Sacred Grove, the Goddess's Magister, and her personal bodyguard — took up positions standing beside and slightly behind her.

As a member of the Black Guard, I stood at attention and tried to ignore the collective weight of their gazes boring into me.

The High Priestess's diamond gaze drifted down my body and I fought to keep my expression blank.

With a sigh, she sat back, lounging on her throne. "What do you think of the new arrival?"

I tried not to frown at the question.

The new arrival, Sage, was stunning and strange, and my shadow had realized something about her that I hadn't figured out yet.

She didn't have the confidence most women had, but her inner strength, her spiritual spark was strong. She hadn't given up or run away when she fell off the rock wall in the sacred pool's chambers. Instead, she'd grabbed that knife off the ground and killed Wells, stopping the unnatural bond forming between them.

My soul said I had to protect her, even if that meant protecting her from myself.

"I don't know her very well, Your Brilliance," I replied, keeping my tone neutral.

The High Priestess turned her attention to her long fingernails. "Come now, Talon. You must have some impression of her."

Oh, I did. And I didn't want to tell the High Priestess. This woman had put Quill through hell and I refused to let her play with Sage.

"She seems shy, Your Brilliance," I said, stating the most obvious thing about the new arrival.

She'd tried to hide her discomfort in the throne room, but it was obvious the attention from the High Priestess and her courtiers had made her uncomfortable.

"She does give off that impression," the High Priestess purred, still staring at her nails. "You're handsome and charming, Talon. I want you to bring her out of her shell."

"Your Brilliance?" I had a bad feeling about this.

"I want you to court her." She snapped her attention to me, locking me in place with her gaze and the threat of power radiating around her. "You've been without a mate for too long."

No.

Oh, hell no.

I loved Quill. I refused to take a female mate unless she was already mated to Quill. Except even then, I couldn't afford to mate her because she and her other mates would find out about my shadow. And if the High Priestess learned I was infected with a shadow entity, she would kill me or send me to the White Tower to be experimented on.

"Your Brilliance, my position in the Black Guard is dangerous."

"Many a guardsman take a mate, Captain Talon, and your term is complete. You can retire your commission at any point." The High Priestess's smile turned cold and calculating. "Your magic is strong. Her magic will be extraordinary. Your child will be a boon to this realm."

My shadow coiled tighter within me, its anxiety and rage suddenly gone as if it were hiding not just from the High Priestess but me as well.

The High Priestess couldn't know for certain that Sage and I would have a child. Her Brilliance was powerful, but she couldn't see into the future — that was a magic so rare it hadn't been seen in generations. Still, I couldn't refuse her because we might not have a child.

I needed something better. At the very least, I needed to stall for time until she found more suitable mates.

"Your Brilliance," I said, "The—"

"The next words out of your mouth better be 'I'd be honored,'" Phoenix, the Lord Commander of the Order and the High Priestess's largest mate, growled, and his hand dropped to the hilt of his longsword.

"Despite her bedraggled appearance," Fen said, a

flicker of his immense magical power snapping around him, "the new arrival is passingly attractive."

"She is," I said, keeping my back straight and refusing to bow to Fen's power. "And I'm very honored. I'm just—"

"Are you questioning Her Brilliance's wisdom?" Phoenix added. "Her insight comes straight from the Goddess."

Shit. This was quickly spiraling out of control.

"Lady Sage is traumatized from her attack," I said before the High Priestess's mates could interrupt me again. "As shy as she is, I'm concerned aggressively courting her would fail to win a mating bond."

"That's why you're perfect for the job," the High Priestess said. "Your duties at the Black Tower will ensure you won't be able to court her nightly, giving her time to adjust. I can make no guarantee that the rest of my court will be as sensitive to her situation."

"If they're not sensitive, they won't win her heart, Your Brilliance," I said, the words leaping out before I could stop them.

The High Priestess jerked forward her power eclipsing Fen's, squeezing around my chest, and stealing my breath.

"In her condition, she's easily manipulated," she hissed. "You will make her mate with you by the end of next season, or you won't be around to mate with anyone, ever."

Her power shoved me to my knees and bent me forward, pressing my forehead to the cold marble floor.

Fuck fuck fuck. I couldn't do that to Sage. I couldn't do that to anyone. But if I didn't, I was dead.

CHAPTER 18
Rider

THE THRONE ROOM'S heavy doors slammed shut behind me, the sound echoing through the ornate hallway. My wolf heaved inside me, not wanting to leave Sage with Quill and West — a man who I didn't know and didn't trust — but I had no choice.

I couldn't challenge the High Priestess. She'd made her decision and there was nothing I could do about it.

A growl rumbled in my throat, making Ash, Onyx, and Zinnia, look at me, questions in their eyes.

She's not my Goddess-damned mate.

She's not.

But I hated that she'd been in danger, *was still* in danger, and that the High Priestess had taken a liking to her.

I didn't know how Her Brilliance had heard so quickly about the attack, but I didn't like it. She was a powerful leader, used to dealing with human men who looked down on her, and she liked being in control.

But she also had a wicked streak, especially with people who she thought were useful, and clearly from her mention of Sage's magic, she thought Sage was useful.

Thankfully, Quill had diverted the conversation before Sage was forced to reveal her magic in public, but unfortunately, with the High Priestess taking an interest in her, Sage was going to be the talk of not just the Garden, but the whole court, possibly beyond. And not just unmated men would be interested in her. Everyone would be.

Goddess. Even with our few brief encounters, I knew Sage was shy.

The kind of attention she was going to receive now would be torture. And the High Priestess was going to enjoy watching her squirm before coming to rescue her from the situation she had intentionally created.

I led us down the hall, away from the knight stationed at the door and any other prying eyes and glanced at Ash. His scarred face was an impassive mask, and he acted as if it didn't matter that Sage had been taken into the Divine Residence where he couldn't follow her.

But I knew him too well, and the rigid set of his shoulders and the tightness around his dark eyes betrayed his inner turmoil.

The question was: did he fear not being able to court her because he couldn't reach her in the Divine Residence or did he think she'd reject him once the stress of the situation had worn off?

And with my wolf heaving inside me, straining to rip through my fae form, I couldn't focus enough to figure out which it was.

"I hope she doesn't keep Talon," Onyx murmured as soon as we were out of earshot from the guards.

"I hope he doesn't require Flint's healing," I growled back.

Zinnia's eyebrows rose in surprise, making me wonder if she knew about Her Brilliance's proclivities.

I doubted the High Priestess would punish Talon for Sage's attack. She was more likely to hurt him to keep riding the pleasure she got from playing with Sage. And while Talon was sometimes up for a little pain with his pleasure, it had to be with the right person. The High Priestess and her mates were not the right people.

My vision shifted to my wolf's sight, and I squeezed the bridge of my nose to keep him at bay.

Protect. Mate. Mine.

Fuck.

There was too much going on and my wolf was losing his mind. Hell, there'd been too much before Ash had told us Wells and Crane had attacked Sage. I hadn't wanted anything to do with the new arrival, no matter how much she haunted me, and now I couldn't stop thinking about her.

And she sure as hell *wasn't* my mate.

My thoughts leaped to her conversation with Zinnia. The door to the bedroom had been closed, but my wolf enhanced my hearing and I hadn't been able to stop listening to their words.

"You've been raised in the human realm." Zinnia's words had frozen everything within me and I jumped to the same conclusion she had, that Sage was a slave.

I'd wanted Sage to deny it. She could have just been raised by humans. It explained why she reminded me so much of Isemay. But in the next breath, she'd confirmed some human was holding her captive and abusing her.

I'd wanted to tear the door down and vow I'd protect her and the human boy she was helping. Both my wolf and I were in agreement that she couldn't stay where she was. But if she was as like Isemay as I suspected, she'd never tell someone she didn't trust. She certainly wouldn't tell someone because they demanded to know.

No, if I wanted to rescue Sage and the boy, I needed to earn her trust. Letting my feral instincts take over wasn't going to help, no matter how hard it currently was to keep my wolf in check.

"Lord Commander Rider," a sharp, masculine voice called out behind me.

I jerked to a stop and glared at the knight rushing toward us.

"What?" my wolf snarled through my lips.

The knight stumbled to a stop, his eyes wide. Two more knights drew up behind him, keeping enough distance between them as if they hoped my wolf's ire would remain focused on the man in front of him.

"Lord Commander Phoenix requires your presence in his office," the knight squeaked. "Captain Ash and Sir Onyx as well."

I huffed. I doubted Phoenix was so polite. He'd sent—

I glanced at the knight's collar for his rank. Captain. The man cowering before the threat of my wolf was a knight captain.

And the men behind him were both sergeants.

Clearly, they weren't making Order Knights like the used to.

"I have a text I need to consult, but I'll head to Sage's suite shortly," Zinnia assured me.

I gave her a tight nod and turned back to our escort. "Lead the way, captain."

He stumbled back a step before turning and hurrying down the hall.

The sergeants waited until Ash, Onyx, and I had passed before following behind us.

I huffed again at their foolishness. I wasn't going to resist a command from the High Priestess's knights and just the three of them wouldn't have been able to stop me if my wolf got out of control.

The captain led us down the long corridors to the north wing where the Order was stationed inside the Residence — a path all of us knew well — and into the sitting room outside the Lord Commander's office.

The north wing and the Lord Commander's sitting room lacked the luxury found in the rest of the corridors and rooms in the Divine Residence. The furnishings and features were finer than anything the Black Guard had, but compared to everything else for the High Priestess, it was plain and utilitarian.

Which, ironically, was very much like the Lord Commander of the Order of the Sacred Grove himself. Phoenix was a skilled, dangerous, practical warrior. He was older than me by a century and had been the deputy commander of the Order when he mated the soon-to-be High Priestess.

He was a competent commander but also completely dedicated to his mate. Which meant he'd take Sage's safety seriously, but if the High Priestess wanted to play with Sage, he'd allow it and no one could stop it. Her Brilliance would think that just by saving Sage, we were interested in her, and we could get roped into whatever game she was playing.

CHAPTER 19
Rider

ASH AND ONYX sat on the wooden bench in the Lord Commander's sitting room that ran along the side of the wall, while I paced from Phoenix's closed office door to the open door leading to the hall and back again.

There was no point in even trying to sit. My wolf was too agitated. It needed to hunt down the rest of the men who'd attacked Sage and find her, wherever she was in the Residence. It didn't want Phoenix to waste its time and draw it into something political.

Minutes later — that felt like hours to my wolf — Phoenix strode into the sitting room.

"I don't have a lot of time." He marched across the room to his office.

Ash shot me a glance, his expression wary, while Onyx hurried to follow.

A part of me cursed myself for getting my sister's mate mixed up in this. Phoenix was his commanding officer, and Onyx could be in a world of trouble, but there wasn't anyone else in the Order who I trusted.

I strode into the room with Ash a step behind me and dropped into one of the leather highbacked chairs in front of his desk. My wolf heaved under my skin, but I forced it down and feigned a calm I didn't feel.

Phoenix couldn't know how I felt and I couldn't let him think he was superior to me. He wasn't. We were both Lord Commanders of elite forces — and as much as everyone looked down on the Black Guard because half of the army was human, they *were* a highly trained force. And in the area of actual combat, I was the more experienced warrior.

Ash took position standing to my right and slightly behind the chair, while Onyx strode to the front of Phoenix's desk and stood at attention. Phoenix dropped into the chair behind his desk, pushed a pile of papers to the side, and leaned forward.

"Explain exactly what happened," he commanded.

I summarized the situation, knowing Onyx could fill him in on the details.

"So the Great Rider let some of the assailants get away," Phoenix huffed, making my wolf's hackles rise.

"We prioritized the new arrival's safety," Ash said. "We—"

"I didn't ask for your input, Captain." Phoenix's lips curled back in disgust.

Fucking asshole.

I resisted the urge to grow claws and rip off his face. There were too many healers in the Residence so he wouldn't scar, and injuring him would piss off the High Priestess, which would create problems for me and my entire command.

It was bad enough Ash couldn't follow Sage into the Residence because his appearance was too unsightly for Her Brilliance's precious sensibilities. Pissing off Phoenix now could get me, Talon, and Quill banned from the Residence, and then we'd have no way of protecting Sage.

"Her Brilliance wants my best man on this." Pheonix sat back, his gaze locked with mine. "This new arrival is precious to her and the rest of us. That's why she assigned Sir West to Lady Sage's protection."

His words were meant as a peace offering. But they did nothing to ease the fear and anger churning inside me.

Sure, he'd take Sage's protection seriously. But only if he and the High Priestess hadn't been involved in the attack in the first place.

Once I learned who his investigator was, I'd know the truth.

Phoenix's eyes narrowed. "Don't get in my investigator's way."

My wolf snarled back at him before I could stop it, and Phoenix's lips curled with the hint of a wicked smile.

Fuck. He thought I was interested in mating Sage. Which meant the High Priestess would think I was interested in mating Sage.

And I was *not* interested in mating, damn it!

"Dismissed," he said to me before turning his attention to Onyx. "Your report, Captain."

Onyx squared his shoulders and I stormed out of Phoenix's office with Ash at my heels.

Onyx would be fine. He had Phoenix's trust, and Phoenix knew I'd only gone to Onyx because he was family. And if I told myself that enough times, maybe I'd believe it.

Still. I needed to find my sister and let her know what was going on.

We left the north wing, taking a side door into the Garden and hurrying away from prying eyes and ears again.

I led Ash to a secluded nook that was partially hidden by flowering vines, where dim lighting obscured anyone inside and the lights in the Garden beyond made it easy to observe anyone nearby.

"We need a plan," I said, keeping my voice low even though my wolf couldn't sense anyone nearby.

"We need more information," Ash shot back. "We don't know how deep the corruption goes. Does it stop with whoever was supposed to guard the sacred pool or are Phoenix and the High Priestess involved?"

I didn't want to believe the High Priestess would arrange for a woman to be forcibly mated. It went against everything we, as fae, believed in. But Wells, Crane, Thunder, and Addax all had powerful magic. If the High Priestess wanted their loyalty for something, arranging for them to mate would be a way to get them in her debt.

"Do you know anything about West?" I asked.

"Not much. He has personal enhancement magic and it's powerful. He can make himself stronger, faster, more durable, and more agile than naturally possible," Ash replied. "Only Phoenix and a few of his captains can win a fight against him and not consistently."

So if Sage was in trouble, West was more than capable of protecting her. But only if West wasn't a part of that trouble.

My wolf thrashed against my control, furious and desperate. It didn't matter that Quill, a highly skilled swordsman, was with her. It didn't matter that my wolf knew Quill would use every dirty trick he'd learned in the Gray to protect Sage. *It* needed to protect her, too.

Except going right now would draw more of the High Priestess's attention and neither me nor my wolf wanted that. Attention from anyone only increased how much danger Sage was in.

"One of us needs to be with her at all times," I growled.

Ash dipped his head, letting his hair veil the ruined side of his face. "It'll be up to you and Quill."

Fuck. If West didn't let Sage out of the Residence, Ash couldn't be with her, and Talon couldn't take a shift because he couldn't risk being mated to her. She wouldn't understand the nature of his shadow and the High Priestess could execute him if she learned the truth.

Talon and Ash would have to support us by taking up the slack in the Black Tower.

"At least Sage said she only manifests in the Garden at night," Ash added. "Hopefully, it stays that way and it won't interfere with the novice training."

"Or we teach her how to control her manifesting."

New arrivals often struggled with controlling when and how they manifested in the Garden, and from what Sage had said, it sounded like she had that problem. But if we could teach her how to control it, she could avoid the Garden until it was safe.

Goddess, that would make everything so much easier.

Everything except earning her trust and figuring out where she was in the human realm.

My wolf internally snarled and clawed, and I paced to the back of the nook, needing to take action, move, do something!

"You and Quill can work out the details for guard duty tomorrow morning." Ash watched me march back to the nook's opening. "Right now you need to let Lark talk to your wolf."

My wolf opened my mouth to tell Ash I was fine, but I snapped it shut before the words came out. I wasn't fine. I hadn't been fine even before Sage had been attacked.

"Quill said the magister was going to meet him at the entrance to the Sacred Grove," I said. "Talon was supposed to meet him."

"I'll wait for Talon there. If he doesn't show, I'll tell the magister that Sage is in the Residence. He'll be able to find her if he asks a servant." Ash pulled his hair forward again.

I hadn't seen him hide this much when it was just us since the first time he manifested in the Garden and he'd realized his spirit form was scarred like his physical form.

"Once that's taken care of, I'll return to the sacred pool," Ash said.

"Good idea." I was great at noticing scents and following prey, but Ash was the tracker and spymaster of the Black Tower. There was a chance he'd find something I missed. Something whichever knight was assigned to the investigation might miss. "I'll join you."

His dark eyes narrowed.

"After I talk with Lark," I added, and not just

because I needed her to help my wolf calm the fuck down.

By now, she'd have heard about Onyx being summoned to the throne room, and without a doubt, she'd have questions. It was only fair I answered some of them.

I left Ash in the nook and went in search of Lark. By now, Dale's concert was over, but given how Talon had summoned Onyx and that Onyx was probably still with Phoenix, I doubted my sister and her other mates had gone to the after-concert celebration. They were probably worried.

A flicker of guilt soured the taste in my mouth. I didn't want to worry my sister. She was distressed enough at trying to get pregnant, and added worry about her mate wouldn't help her situation.

But there wasn't anything I could do about it, and I wouldn't have done anything different. Sage had needed to talk to someone I trusted, someone who I knew wouldn't scare her, and Onyx had been the man for the job.

I found Lark in a private sitting room at the edge of the east wing of the Residence. Plush furniture and lush greenery filled the luxurious space, and the air was thick with the scent of blooming flowers. The relaxing smell stood in stark contrast to the tension radiating through the room, and my guilt churned my stomach.

Lark sat curled on a velvet couch with Flint and Dale on either side of her, while Blaze furiously paced the room. The tiger shifter's gaze jumped to the entrance the moment I stepped into sight.

With a snarl, he leaped at me, grabbed the front of my leather tunic and heaved me inside. "What the hell is going on? If Onyx is in trouble—"

My wolf surged forward, and I shoved Blaze back. Blinding fury roared through me and my consciousness was shoved aside. I threw myself at him, my spirit form tearing apart and reforming into my wolf.

If Onyx was in trouble I'd protect him like I'd protect Talon, Quill, and Ash. Something hurting Onyx hurt my sister and neither me nor my wolf would stand for that.

Hell, I'd even protect Blaze no matter how much I wanted to kill him right now.

Flint yelled something, but I couldn't hear him past the rushing in my ears.

Mine. Mine mine mine.

The word kept ringing in my ears over and over again.

Blaze scrambled away from me, his tiger flashing bright gold in his shocked amber eyes. Between the two of us, he usually lost control first, but my wolf just couldn't take it anymore. It *needed* to hunt, to kill, to protect.

It had lost its fucking mind. The novices were out

of control, the childish men in the Garden were out of control, and the High Priestess liked to play games my wolf couldn't control. It needed something solid and certain within its grasp and it had ridiculously — foolishly, childishly, insanely, please Goddess only temporarily — decided Sage was how it was going to regain control.

And it didn't have time to fuck around with Blaze. It had to ensure Sage was safe. Now now now.

I lunged, forcing Blaze back until he hit the wall, then surged forward. I shifted back into my human form and pinned him against the wall with a clawed hand at this throat.

"Enough!" Lark screamed.

My wolf leaned closer to Blaze to ensure he'd stay put then looked at my sister.

"Enough, Rider," she repeated, her tone softening as a thread of her magic wrapped around me and whispered directly with the wolf spark buried in the core of my being.

I didn't know what was said, only that my wolf huffed and jerked me away from Blaze.

My wolf was still on edge, still desperate for a fight, but somehow Lark had convinced it to trust me. I would give it a fight. But we needed to fight the right people, and Blaze wasn't one of those people.

CHAPTER 20
Sage

I CLUNG to Quill's arm to keep my balance as we left the throne room, and the servant led us down a hall just as majestic as the wide hall as the one before. Intricate patterns swirled through the stone and wood walls, and ornate chandeliers hung above with their unwavering fae lights.

I clutched my blanket tighter around my shoulders, trying to steady my trembling hands and pretend I wasn't on the brink of falling apart. But the weight of everything pressed down on me threatened to crush what little composure I had left.

I needed a moment alone, somewhere safe where I could gather my thoughts and try to make sense of this nightmare.

But safety was an illusion. In the Black Tower and here.

I had more than enough proof of that.

"It's so exciting to have you here in the Garden, my lady," the servant said, his tone overly cheerful. "Such a shame about that nasty attack, but don't you worry one bit. The knights will take care of everything. They're simply the best, they're—" The servant glanced back at Lord Quill, his eyes widening. "My apologies, Your Highness. The Black Guard is excellent too, of course. Just... different, what with the humans and all."

Your Highness? My gaze jerked to Lord Quill despite my determination not to look at him, and the magnetic pull I always felt toward him captured me. He was so close I could feel the heat from his body and his arm was solid and strong beneath my fingers, supporting me.

I needed to put distance between us before I did something stupid, but letting go of his arm would be rude. Especially if Lord Quill *was* royalty in the fae realm. And in all honesty, I needed him to keep me from stumbling.

"It's Captain," Lord Quill corrected without noticing me staring at him.

The servant's face flushed. "Right, of course. My apologies, Captain."

Without another word, the servant led us to a winding staircase that curled around an enormous tree trunk. Above, strange structures were built onto the massive boughs.

The minstrels told tales about the magic of the fae court, and not a single one I'd heard came close to describing the real thing. I'd known that the Garden was beautiful and magical. I'd thought the grove, with its mix of stone and foliage and its curling flowering vines, was amazing. But the castle in the great tree was beyond imagination.

We followed wide branches — each step making my stomach lurch as I tried not to look down — and swinging bridges connecting different sections.

I gripped Quill's arm tighter, terrified of making a wrong step, and his free hand rested over mine, a gesture so natural and comforting it made my heart ache.

"Are you all right?" he asked softly, his green gaze searching my face, his eyes narrowing when it passed over my bruised cheek.

I heaved my attention away from him, afraid if I spoke, I'd confess how much his touch both soothed and terrified me, and that I craved him even though he'd already proven I couldn't trust him.

"Fine," I forced out before snapping my mouth shut and stopping any other words from escaping.

Two more flights of stairs brought us to another hall. This one was simpler than the main halls below, but just as elegant. It stretched over three hundred feet before ending at a T intersection, and six doors lined the walls, three on each side.

The servant stopped at the middle door on the right and opened it with a flourish.

"Your chambers, my lady," he announced.

Inside was a lavish room with a seating area that consisted of intricately carved, plush furniture sitting by a roaring fire crackling in an enormous marble fireplace, a dining area for six, and a small office nook with a desk and an empty bookshelf. Tapestries depicting lush forests and magical creatures adorned the walls, their threads shimmering in the firelight, and heavy rugs cushioned the floor.

Two partially open doors stood on either side of the room, revealing one lavish bedroom with an enormous bed draped in silks and furs, large enough to comfortably fit Lark and her four mates. The other room was a much plainer bedroom with simple furnishings and a single-person bed.

The High Priestess had said I'd have to share the suite with Sir West. I wasn't sure which bedroom was supposed to be mine, but I couldn't imagine the hulking Sir West fitting in the single-person bed.

Before I could ask which room was mine, the servant bustled past me to the back of the sitting room and threw open a set of large glass doors, revealing a balcony.

Beyond the balcony's railing, lights twinkled in the windows of rooms sitting on other branches and flickered through gently swaying leaves. The vine with the softly glowing pink and white flowers that was everywhere trailed over the balcony's railing and up the side of the building, the illumination from the flowers dancing softly in the gentle breeze.

I stepped out onto the balcony, taking in the dazzling view. Below, the manicured lawn of the Garden stretched out toward a barely lightening horizon. Lights dotted here and there, illuminating small seating areas and secluded nooks as well as the reflection pool where I always found myself when I woke in the Garden.

I swallowed, my mouth suddenly dry. Wells and Crane had known I'd always manifested there, and I always manifested lying down and slowly woke. How many of the other men involved in my attack knew I always appeared there?

How many men in general knew?

A shudder swept through me, and I jerked away from the balcony and hurried back into the sitting room. I never wanted to wake there alone and exposed again.

Someone knocked on the door, and Sir West's hand shifted to the hilt of one of the massive swords hanging at his hips.

The servant opened it, and another servant entered carrying a tray with a softly glowing sphere the size of a coin nestled on top of a thick white velvet square. The servant dropped to his knees, his head bowed, and held up the tray. "Your spirit anchor, my lady."

I stared at him. The white light from the sphere illuminated his refined features. I didn't know what a spirit anchor was and I didn't want to touch it.

Except I had no doubt refusing would upset the High Priestess.

"If you would be so kind as to press your finger against it?" the first servant said, gesturing to the sphere after my too-long hesitation.

I *really* didn't want to touch it.

It was going to control me in some way, and I couldn't afford to be captured.

Of course, if the magister Lord Quill had asked to help remove the bracelet currently keeping my spirit trapped in the Garden couldn't free me, being controlled by this spirit anchor wouldn't matter. I'd be discovered in my room in the Gray... it would just be a matter of if I was discovered before or after my body died from lack of food or lack of a spirit.

"My lady," the first servant said. "Sir West will protect it so you'll only ever manifest in his presence. You have nothing to worry about."

I had everything to worry about.

Great Father, this was a nightmare. Sure I wasn't going to wake up by that pond anymore. I was going to wake up beside that monster. For all I knew, the High

Priestess could be forcing me into the hands of the men who wanted to hurt me.

And I had no choice.

If I refused, everyone would be suspicious of me, and I had no idea what would happen then.

With a slow breath to steady my nerves and hopefully not reveal how upset I was, I placed my finger against the small sphere.

The soft white glow turned red, the same color as my hair, then it released a bright flash, sending black specks dancing through my vision, before dimming back to its original brightness.

The color, however, remained red, proof that I was now trapped by whoever controlled the stone.

The servant, still kneeling, turned his raised tray to Sir West, offering him the anchor. West took it and the velvet square, which was actually a small velvet bag with long, delicate golden ties. He hung it around his neck, slipping it inside his armor where it was impossible for me, or anyone else, to reach.

With deep bows, both servants left, and Sir West closed the door behind them. The latch clicked, the sound too loud in my ears, and I fought to control my breathing.

I could handle this. I *had* to handle this.

Perhaps Sir West was a good man.

Except he obeyed the High Priestess and I was a mouse for her to play with.

Just like how there was a chance the King of Erellod could have been involved in my stepfather's plans to send Sawyer to the Gray, the High Priestess could have been involved in Wells's and Crane's plans to forcibly bond with me.

CHAPTER 21
Sage

SIR WEST TURNED AWAY from the door and glared at Quill while Quill watched me, his emerald gaze intense.

I squirmed under his scrutiny. "So if I always manifest in the Garden where the spirit anchor is and you always have the anchor," I said to Sir West. "Why do we need to be spirit linked?"

"For added protection, my lady," Sir West said, his voice deep and harsh.

"Once the immediate threat is gone, you'll be able to secure the anchor in your suite here," Lord Quill said, drawing my gaze back to him. "Right now, the High Priestess believes you're safest if you're always with Sir West." The muscles in Quill's jaw flexed. He didn't believe what he just said.

The realization made me even more nervous to be stuck with Sir West.

I really needed to figure out how to stop waking in the Garden. If I could do that, this whole mess wouldn't matter. Zinnia had said she'd find me, and I was sure I could ask her about controlling when and where I manifested.

Although I suspected it was going to be the same as changing my clothes. Just imagine it and it'll happen.

Which was easier said than done.

Sudden, desperate heat flared around my neck, and a violent achy need clawed at my insides as if my mating marks hadn't been put to sleep. The force drew a sharp gasp and a tremble swept through me, threatening my balance.

Oh, Father!

Sir West jerked toward me as if to grab me, but Lord Quill reached me first, steadying me with firm hands on my hips.

The power that always snapped between us when we touched stole my breath, and my soul burned for him, ramping up my need.

"I've got you," he murmured, his warm breath feathering over the back of my neck. "Let me help you."

Yes. Oh, yes yes yes.

I ached for him, every fiber of my being screamed to give in. But I couldn't let him see my marks. He'd ask questions. He'd wonder if he was the mate his goddess had picked for me when Zinnia had said some of my marks turning green might not mean I had a mate.

Except how much of that was just to console me? Zinnia knew I didn't want a mate. She'd seen my panic at the thought that my soul was bound to someone else's. Maybe she'd lied and I really was permanently bound to a fae man.

"I'm fine," I insisted, my voice breathy with need.

I couldn't give in. The spike of desire would pass. I could last until Zinnia got here and...

And I had no idea what I'd do after that. I had questions, but Zinnia arriving didn't mean the ache within me would instantly go away.

Another hot spike roared through me, and I bit my lip to stop the moan that bubbled in my throat.

"You're not fine." Quill's grip on my hips tightened and he pressed close, his chest against my back. "Let me take care of you. I don't have magic. The Goddess won't bond us."

Yes.

No.

Damn it. I couldn't trust him.

Whatever it was that zinged between us was a lie. My body craving him didn't mean anything.

"I just need to rest." I yanked out of his hold and stumbled forward.

Sir West took another jerky step toward me, his

hands held out to catch me as if he thought I was going to collapse.

"No." I held up a hand, stopping him before he could reach me. "I'm *fine*."

"You're not," Lord Quill insisted. "The pressure from your marks is going to keep getting stronger."

I wanted to tell him it wouldn't, that Zinnia had put my marks to sleep and I just needed to wait for this desire spike to pass. But I didn't want to deal with the inevitable questions.

Except from his expression, he wasn't going to give up.

Fine. If he was going to insist I be with someone—

"I want Ash," I trusted Ash more than I trusted anyone else. He might be a Captain of the Black Guard and beholden to Rider's commands, but my very essence told me I was safe with him.

Quill's concern shifted to something strange and sad that I couldn't recognize. "Captain Ash isn't permitted in this part of the Divine Residence."

"Not permitted?" Except I had a horrible feeling I knew why he wasn't permitted.

"Captain Ash isn't pretty enough," Sir West stated, his expression darkening even more making it obvious he wasn't pretty enough either. And my best guess as to why he was in the suite now was because he'd been shackled to me.

Was I a punishment for Sir West?

The High Priestess had spirit linked us, did she believe the goddess wouldn't bond us together?

Or did she believe we would be bound together, and I was a reward.

I shuddered at the thought. The fae's goddess might bind fae together, but that didn't mean the High Priestess couldn't push fate in whatever direction she wanted. All the High Priestess had to do was restrict who I could and couldn't be in contact with. Eventually my mating marks would pick from whoever was available.

I didn't know which was worse, knowing you had no control over your fate like a human woman, or having the illusion of control like a fae woman.

And after my one rotation as a guardsman, I hated not having any control at all. I hated being demure and afraid and obedient. Even as a man magically bound to the Black Tower I at least felt like I had some control.

"If Ash isn't allowed in the suite," I said. "I'll go to him."

If they were so determined to make me have sex with someone, it was going to be with the one man in this place I actually trusted.

Sir West stiffened. "It isn't safe."

Of course it wasn't. Logically I knew that. Some of the men who'd attacked me were still out there, but everything this evening had been out of my control. Wells and Crane had abducted me, my marks had flared making me desperate, and the High Priestess had bound me to Sir West.

"So I'm a prisoner?" I snapped.

Oh, shit!

My stomach bottomed out, and I slapped a hand over my mouth to stop myself from saying more. I couldn't risk making Sir West angry... or any angrier than he already was.

"Not at all," Quill said with a quick glance at Sir West whose expression remained solidly grim. "But until we— until *the Order*," he corrected himself, "can identify everyone involved in the attack, you're safer in this suite."

Father! He sounded like every human man I'd come across.

And I felt like I always did. Trapped, helpless, afraid.

There wasn't any difference between being a human woman and a fae woman.

Sir West would undoubtedly stop me from leaving, and even if I managed to escape, the soul link would tell him exactly where I was.

I swallowed at the bitter taste in my mouth and blinked back the tears of frustration burning my eyes.

"I shall retire to my room," I forced out, straining to keep my voice soft and even.

I dropped my gaze to my feet. I didn't have the strength to lift it. My whole life I'd been taught to bow to the men around me and in the face of utter defeat, I couldn't resist the compulsion.

I turned to the bedroom with the simple one-person bed, but Lord Quill, his hands still on my hips, directed me toward the fancy bedroom.

A hysterical laugh bubbled in my throat and I fought to swallow it back. The enormous bed was mine? Sir West was going to have to squeeze into that tiny bed for however long we were stuck together?

Clearly I wasn't a reward for the monstrous knight.

I squared my shoulders fighting to regain whatever dignity I had left and strode toward the fancy bedroom. But Sir West followed me, his footsteps heavy and ominous.

He wasn't going to leave me alone.

He wasn't going to stay in that tiny bed.

No.

No way in hell.

I needed a god-damned moment to myself, time to pull myself together, relieve the pressure from my mating marks, and sob my heartache and frustration in a pillow.

He was *not* going to watch me do that.

"By myself, my lord," I said with as firm a tone as I could manage.

Please. I just need a moment.

Another spike of desire slammed into me, and I

clenched every muscle in my body to stay standing and hide my reaction.

"I've been ordered to guard you," he rumbled. "I can't let you out of my sight."

Of course he couldn't.

"I'm just going to rest in bed."

"My lady," he insisted, sending a shock of rage surging through me.

I. Needed. A. Moment.

"So what?" I spun on him, all fear of being reprimanded gone. Whatever he came up with to punish me couldn't be as bad as running the trail until I threw up or being beaten every few days, or watching my brother on the ground desperate to breathe. "You're going to watch everything?"

Sir West stared at me grimly.

"When I bathe? When I make love? Even when I piss?"

"Your safety until you've bound all your mates is my only duty."

"West," Lord Quill said, stepping between us.

Sir West glared at him. "My *only* duty."

Another spike of need, this one overwhelming, crashed through me, and my knees gave out. I hit the floor hard, gasping and shivering, and both Sir West and Lord Quill lurched toward me.

Quill shouldered West out of the way — something Sir West had to have allowed given that I doubted anyone could have moved the man if he set his mind to it.

"Let me take care of you," Quill begged, cupping my face in his hands.

My pulse pounded, and the sincerity in his green eyes made my soul ache for him.

A part of me desperately wanted him, was certain he was mine. Maybe he was my mate, the reason some of my marks turned green.

"Please let me help you," he said again.

My arguments for keeping him at a distance because I didn't want him to see my magicless marks and because I didn't trust him started to crumble.

He and the others were going to see my marks at some point. They were going to ask questions regardless, and Quill obeying Lord Rider didn't mean much if I wasn't going to get attached to him.

And I wasn't going to get attached.

I'd been fine having sex with Ash and not knowing his name, understanding that we weren't building a relationship and just having fun. I'd be fine using Lord Quill to ease the desire from my marks.

And if I thought that enough times, maybe I'd eventually believe it.

Zinnia had said it could take days or even months for the desire in my marks to completely go away. If the spikes were this strong, I wouldn't last.

I'd lose my mind if it took months.

Hell, I'd lose my mind if it took days.

And what if it followed me back to the Gray?

If Talon's desire was added to it—

I shuddered. I didn't want to think about it.

I had to get my need under control. I had to control something, anything. And if I was being honest with myself, I'd craved Lord Quill from the moment he'd ridden into the Herstind Castle's bailey.

CHAPTER 22
Quill

"PLEASE," I begged Sage. "Let me help you."

Goddess.

I squeezed my eyes shut. I was losing my mind. That same shock of something I'd felt when I'd touched Sawyer's sister zinged through me as if the woman in front of me was actually the human woman who I'd unknowingly left behind in danger.

My vision had even wavered as I'd stood behind her in the throne room. One moment I saw Sage, the newest arrival to the Garden, her red hair falling in tangled waves down her back. The next, she was Sawyer's sister, her face pale with shock because I'd said her brother's name.

I forced my eyes open to look at the *fae* woman in front of me. I couldn't let my longing for a woman I didn't even know affect how I reacted to Sage. They both had red hair... and perhaps a similarly shaped face, but that was all. It was a passing resemblance that my mind was trying to make into more than it was.

And the *fae* woman needed me thinking clearly.

She still had the blanket clutched tight around her neck, and her cheek was still stained with a vivid purple bruise. My soul screamed to protect her, to gather her in my arms and never let go, that she was mine to take care of. But she couldn't be mine because I didn't have any magic. That, and I felt this same urgent need with Sawyer's sister.

She wasn't mine.

Never mine.

But I still had to help. She trembled with unful-filled desire and there was no way I was letting West ease the pressure from her marks.

I glanced at the knight, his posture rigid and his expression stony. I'd pushed him aside to get to Sage when she'd collapsed on the floor. But he had to have let me push him, which meant he either didn't want to get personally involved or respected the higher rank I used to have.

He was younger than me and had joined the Order of the Sacred Grove after I'd joined the Black Guard so we'd never met. Rumors claimed he was withdrawn even amongst his fellow knights and that he was inca-pable of smiling.

Of course, people said the same thing about Rider,

and I knew that wasn't true. Rider was just very selective with whom he shared his smile.

That said, a similarity to Rider didn't mean I could trust West, and until we uncovered everyone involved in Wells's plot against Sage, everyone was a suspect.

Even my mother.

I shuddered at the thought. She was clearly playing games by soul linking Sage and West, which, from the hushed words of the courtiers, had surprised everyone, not just me.

Given West's plain appearance, I hadn't thought my mother liked West enough to try to mate him to Sage, but that was what it looked like she was doing.

Had my mother struck a bargain with Wells and Crane? Had she promised Sage to them? It wouldn't surprise me if my mother had struck some kind of deal with them.

Sage shivered and her breathing picked up. A strangled moan escaped her lips, wrenching me from my worries back to the immediate problem. I hadn't seen her marks since the rescue, but they had glowed unnaturally bright. The pressure from them to have sex had to be overwhelming.

That had to be why she'd been hiding them in the throne room. She didn't want people thinking they could take advantage of her in her vulnerable state.

Someone had to help her, and since it couldn't be Ash, it had to be me.

"Stay in the sitting room," I said in my sternest voice to West. "I'll take care of Sage."

Sage bowed her head, but thankfully didn't protest.

"I'm not letting her leave my sight." West took a step closer, his massive form towering over me with me crouched in front of Sage. Hell, his form towered over me when I was standing, too.

"The lady has started her hunt and needs relief," I insisted.

"By all means," West rumbled, gesturing to the bed in the lavish bedroom.

Except Ash had made it perfectly clear that Sage was shy and nervous around men. She hadn't gone to the courtyard like the other women. It was obvious she didn't want the attention. I doubted she was an exhibitionist and wanted someone watching. It wasn't typical behavior among women, but it wasn't unheard of, either.

"Sir West," I said, standing and squaring my shoulders.

It didn't matter that West stood a head taller than me. I was pulling rank.

"As my mother's son, I command you to wait in the sitting room while I attend to Lady Sage." I met his brilliant sapphire gaze. "With the door closed."

Goddess, I hated pulling rank, especially when I no longer truly held any rank of note in the High Priestess's court. But for some reason, people still recognized me as the High Priestess's son, despite her public rejection of me the moment I discovered I didn't have any magic.

The muscles in West's jaw flexed, the only indication of an emotion beyond grim acceptance.

I cocked an eyebrow, waiting for his response and praying he'd bow to my authority.

Being the son of the High Priestess didn't really mean much since the goddess selected the next High Priestess, but more often than not at least one of the High Priestess's sons was mated to her replacement. And mate to the High Priestess was the second most powerful position in court.

West kept staring.

"Sir West," I huffed. "I helped rescue Sage. I'm not a threat, not physically and not spiritually. I'm also more than capable of protecting her long enough for you to break down the door and give aid."

West grunted and his gaze dipped ever so slightly, breaking our stare-off.

I took that as permission, dropped back into a crouch before Sage could stand — which it looked like she was trying and failing to do — and swept her into my arms. She trembled against me as I carried her into the large bedroom with the massive bed and shut the door with a gentle kick.

This guest suite was one of the finest in the Divine Residence. It had opulent furnishings, an amazing view of the Garden, and a luxurious bathing room. And it made my stomach churn. Sage had captured my mother's attention and nothing good ever came from that.

I could only pray my mother would grow bored of this particular game before Sage got hurt.

As carefully as I could, I laid Sage on the bed. Her grip on the blanket had slipped when she'd tried to stand, and now I could see some of her marks.

My pulse stalled.

Not a hint of magic flickered within them. They were flat, lifeless.

My gaze leaped to hers and for a moment all I could see were shocked brown eyes flecked with impossible green.

I had to protect her.

I needed to know she was safe.

It didn't matter that she was human.

My soul wept for her.

Then the green bled over the brown. I stared at Sage again, and the urge to protect her was just as strong as the need to protect Sawyer's sister.

Damn it. Concentrate.

I brushed a finger over her marks near her jaw, making her gasp and jerked back from me.

"Whatever Wells did," she said, her voice strained, "it affected my marks."

My fingers stalled on a green mark.

This one was also lifeless but it had clearly changed from her hair color to her eye color. Had the goddess actually bonded her to Wells?

No, if the goddess had, the mark wouldn't be green. It would have been gray because Wells was dead. Rider had confirmed that. Which meant the goddess had bonded her to someone else.

It had to be Ash.

Sage was closest with him. She'd asked for him when I'd insisted she address her desire, and it had broken my heart to tell her my mother wouldn't allow him in the Residence because of his scars.

A part of me was jealous that Sage would bond with Ash. I'd yearned for a mate for over a century, ached with the need as irrational as that was. That was why I was losing my mind, feeling connected to Sawyer's sister and now Sage. My soul was so desperate that I'd cling to anything even when it wasn't true — in the case of Sawyer's sister — or couldn't happen — in Sage's case.

The churning mix of emotions soured in my mouth. I shouldn't be upset the goddess bonded Sage and Ash. Ash needed a mate. He connected with fae women on a soul-deep level that other fae didn't, and he'd been broken since that horrible night that had scarred him.

But he still had magic. It didn't matter if he wasn't handsome. The goddess didn't care about looks, only that a spark of true love existed and that the man possessed magic.

Except Ash hadn't acted like he was newly bonded. A newly bonded man wouldn't let his mate walk away with two other men into a place he wasn't permitted. He would have insisted going with her and being the one to protect her. When my mother had soul-linked Sage and West, Ash should have completely lost his mind.

Which meant Ash wasn't her mate... or because she didn't have any magic in her marks, the bond wasn't alive and he didn't know.

Sage drew the blanket back over her marks and hugged herself as if that was the only thing holding her together.

"It's all right." I opened my arms, offering her comfort from my body.

She stared at me for so long I was sure she was going to reject me before she sagged forward into my embrace.

"Zinnia put my marks to sleep," she murmured, her voice heartbreakingly soft and uncertain. "I won't find my mates until they reawaken."

I opened my mouth to ask how long that would take, but she shook her head before I could get the words out.

"I don't know when they'll reawaken," she said as if she could read my thoughts. And maybe she could.

I didn't know what magic she possessed, maybe it was mind reading. But even if she couldn't read my thoughts, my question was the next most obvious one. A woman's mating marks were essential. She couldn't mate without them... and she couldn't conceive.

And the High Priestess's fury when she found out would put Sage at risk.

My pulse picked up. I had to protect her.

I hadn't thought her huddled in the blanket, still looking bruised and bedraggled was the best look for an audience in the throne room, but if she couldn't change her spirit clothes, then fully covered had been her safest option.

I glance at the closed bedroom door. The spirit anchor ensured Sage manifested beside West wherever he was. If Sage couldn't change her spirit clothes, he was going to see her marks and tell my mother.

Fuck.

Without a doubt, Sage's spirit was going to return to her body the moment Magister Aster removed the bracelet trapping her in the Garden. Rider needed to know the second after she left. We needed a plan to contain West by either getting him on our side to protect Sage from everyone, including my mother, or finding a way to silence him.

Goddess be damned. I'd thought I was in a nightmare when I saw Sage hanging on the waterfall's jagged rock wall.

"I don't know when they'll reawaken," she said. "Zinnia says a few might have changed color because of the magic she had to use to put them to sleep."

Except I could see in her eyes that she didn't believe that, and she was terrified of what would happen when her marks did reawaken.

I tighten my grip, my body curling around her a little to offer more protection.

For a moment, she stiffened, and my pulse stalled. She was going to reject me even though she needed me. Then she relaxed and leaned her trembling form back into my embrace.

"Zinnia also said I might have desire spikes for a while."

Which explained what was happening now.

"But it'll stop soon," she added.

"Even if your marks were awake, the goddess wouldn't bind our souls together." I shifted so I could look her in the eyes. "It's safe for me to help you through this flare up."

"I know." A mix of fear, yearning, and sadness filled her brown— No, green eyes.

My soul ached for me to be her calm, her shelter, her protection against all the men who would hurt her. I could see the struggle in her gaze, the battle between her desire and her uncertainty. She was strong, yes, but everyone had their breaking point, and she'd reached hers.

"I won't hurt you," I whispered, my voice barely more than a breath, a promise. "I just want to help."

She nodded, a tiny, almost imperceptible movement, but it was enough. It was consent, a fragile trust that I vowed not to shatter.

CHAPTER 23
Quill

SLOWLY, giving her time to pull away if she wanted, I brought my hand up and cupped her cheek. She trembled, but remained frozen where she was, and I traced the line of her jaw with my thumb.

I needed to be careful, extremely careful. I refused to add to her trauma, and while I might not be the one she wanted, I could be a safe place for her to let go.

My other hand mirrored the first, framing her face, and her lips parted slightly in invitation.

I leaned in, again giving her ample time to pull back if she wanted, but she didn't. Instead, she tilted her head up ever so slightly, meeting me halfway.

Our mouths brushed together, a whisper of a touch, and that jolt of something powerful zinged through me. Her breath hitched as if she felt it too, making me afraid she'd stop when I knew she desperately needed the release.

Then a soft moan escaped her lips and she deepened the kiss. I opened for her and our tongues tangled, hers tentative at first before getting bolder, exploring, seeking.

Her hands, which had gripped the blanket, relaxed and moved to my shoulders, pulling me closer. The fabric slipped down, revealing more of her unnatural magicless marks, but I didn't let them distract me. I had to keep my focus on her, her needs and desires, or my anger at what had happened to her would take over.

I shifted so she was propped up against the headboard, knelt beside her, and trailed kisses down her jaw, lingering on the sensitive spot just below her ear. She gasped and arched into me.

"You're safe with me," I murmured against her neck, feeling her pulse race under my lips.

I wanted to promise that I wouldn't let anyone hurt her again, but I couldn't. I didn't have magic and I couldn't protect her the way a man like Rider or Talon could.

Sure, I was skilled with a sword, one of the best in the Black Guard, but I hadn't become the Captain of the White Tower because of my fighting prowess. I'd become captain because I could calm people, negotiate, think clearly in chaotic situations.

If I'd been there when Wells and Crane had attacked, I might have been able to slow them down long enough for Sage to escape, but I wouldn't have been able to completely stop them. Not with both of them having powerful magic.

"Please," she moaned. "I need more."

My heart clenched at the raw need in her voice. Slowly, I pushed the blanket off her shoulders and traced my fingers down her arms to her waist, giving her time to adjust to each new touch, determined not to spook her. When I reached the hem of her damp dress, I paused and looked at her for permission.

"Yes." Her gaze locked with mine, trust and desperate need swirling in their emerald... brown...? depths.

Emerald. Focus.

I slid my hands under her dress, skimming up her cool, smooth thighs, pushing the damp fabric up as I went. She still trembled, and I prayed it was more with anticipation than fear or shock. She knew she needed this, but that didn't mean she was happy about it.

Adjusting to lie beside her, I pressed gentle kisses along the inside of her thighs, pushing her dress up and revealing more and more of her body.

She gasped as I neared her core, and I paused again, giving her one last moment to change her mind and push me away.

"Quill, please," she groaned, her fingers tangling in

my hair, and she parted her thighs, revealing her soft pink core.

Fuck.

She isn't mine. She can't be mine.

I didn't even know her, and I was confusing her for Sawyer's sister. Even now, I could see the human woman in the fae one lying in front of me.

I squeezed my eyes shut.

Relieve her desire and protect her.

Human or fae those were the only two things I needed to think about right now.

I dove between her legs and flicked my tongue against her, drawing a gasp. Her body tensed as if she were afraid to fully surrender, but the desire in her eyes, the need written all over her face, told me she was barely hanging on.

I licked again, tracing her delicate folds and drawing a low, pleading moan that sent shivers down my spine. My cock, already hard, strained against my pants in anticipation. I wanted to bury myself inside her, feel her warmth and tightness envelop me, but I resisted, knowing this moment belonged to her, and her pleasure was my primary concern.

Her breathing grew ragged. She was close with just those quick touches, but with a desire that had been strong enough it had brought her to her knees, I knew this could be fast. Or at least her first release would be. She'd probably need more than one, but I wasn't sure if she trusted me enough to fully satiate her needs.

I gripped her hips, holding her steady, and licked and sucked, my tongue dancing against her sensitive clit, swirling and teasing, driving her closer and closer to the edge. Her moans filled the room, and the urge to make her come, to watch her face contort in bliss, hear her scream my name, was overwhelming.

My cock was so hard it hurt. I hadn't gotten this hard for a woman in years. Hell, I didn't think I'd ever gotten this hard for a woman before. It didn't matter that we could never be mates, or that my soul confused her for a human woman I was obsessing over. I'd only ever gotten this hard for Talon. My soul had only ever really sung for him even though I desperately wanted a mate and a child.

I'd always wanted that. But in the dream, Talon was always also my mate.

I increased the pressure, determined to stay in the moment, and sucked on her clit, my tongue darting and flicking in a relentless rhythm that had her writhing beneath me. Her hips bucked, and I braced an arm across her pelvis to hold her down and thrust two fingers inside her.

"Oh, Fa—!" she gasped, her body shaking on the verge.

"Come for me," I commanded, my voice strained with my own need. "Let go and come."

Her core clenched around my fingers and a scream of pleasure tore from her lips. Liquid need gushed over my tongue and lips, and I lapped it up. I couldn't get enough of her sweet release, and I wanted her to tremble and moan and cling to me like she was right now forever.

I pumped my fingers in and out and flicked my tongue over her clit, drawing out her release for as long as possible, even as I subtly bucked into the bed, desperate to relieve the pressure in my aching cock.

"Oh, Lord Q—" she moaned, her body relaxing beneath me. "Oh, I—"

I gave a final teasing flick of my tongue against her clit, making her twitch, and sat back on my heels. Her expression was pure bliss and satisfaction, and my heart swelled with a mixture of pride and possessiveness.

Except the expression lasted only a few lazy blinks, before a wild need filled her eyes. The look was more ferocious than anything she'd expressed before, even when that spike of desire had crumpled her to the floor.

With a snarl, she threw herself at me, tackling me back onto the bed and straddling my hips. I imagined myself naked, removing my spirit clothes knowing from the desperate look in her eyes that she wouldn't have the patience to undress me.

And she didn't even hesitate. She grabbed my hard

cock, and impaled herself on it, dropping down heavily on my pelvis.

A guttural groan tore from my throat as her tight, slick heat enveloped me all the way down to my base. She was molten, her desire scorching, gripping me like a velvet vise, and lightning snapped through me, blazing straight to my heart and stealing my breath.

Red hair and brown eyes with flecks of impossible green filled my vision.

She didn't give me a moment to adjust to the overwhelming pleasure. Instead, she began to move, her hips rising and falling in a wild, feral rhythm that had her small breasts bouncing and her damp red hair swaying around her.

I had to protect her, please her, be with her.

I gritted my teeth, fighting the urge to come right then and there. She was a goddess, a force of nature, her body taking what it needed from mine. Her hands gripped my shoulders, nails digging in as she rode me hard, her breath coming in ragged gasps and moans.

My heart pounded, my blood roaring in my ears, and I struggled to hold back my release. I needed her to come first, needed to feel her shatter around me before I could let go.

I reached for her small breasts, squeezing and kneading them, rolling her nipples until they were hard, taut peaks.

She whimpered, the green in her eyes flickering to

brown... or was that green? Were her ears rounded? No pointed. This was Sage, not Sawyer's sister.

"Quill," she groaned as she redoubled her efforts, her hips slamming down onto mine with bruising force. I could feel the pressure building inside her, her inner walls fluttering around my cock, her body coiling tighter and tighter.

"Sage," I groaned back.

Sage.

Not Sawyer's sister.

"More, more, more," she moaned like a prayer with each violent rock of her hips.

I thrust back, harder, faster. The need to come, to release both of us from the pressure driving us wild, screamed through me. I slid my hand down her body, my fingers finding her clit, swollen and sensitive, and rubbed tight, fast circles. Her moans turned to gasps, her body shaking as she chased her release, her need consuming her entirely.

Her eyes locked onto mine, wild and untamed, her pupils blown so wide with desire I could barely make out their color. Green. No brown.

Fuck.

Green. Green green green.

She was close, so close. I could see it in her face, feel it in the way her body gripped mine.

And it didn't matter if she was human or fae, my soul had picked. I belonged to her.

"Quill," she screamed, and she convulsed, back arched and head thrown back.

Her inner walls clamped down hard on my cock, her orgasm ripping through her and tearing away the rest of my control.

I seized her hips and thrust into her hard and fast. With a violent pleasure that bordered on pain, I came, my cum shooting hot and fast into her. My orgasm roared endlessly as she continued to ride me, drawing out both our pleasures until there was nothing left but the sound of our ragged breathing and the pounding of our hearts.

The only question now was which *her* did I belong to? The fae woman who couldn't bind my soul? Or the human woman I'd seen once and wouldn't ever see again.

CHAPTER 24
Sage

WHAT WAS WRONG WITH ME? I'd never been so brazen in my life. A woman didn't jump a man and take their pleasure from him without any regard for his needs. They accepted whatever he graciously gave them.

But the first orgasm Lord Quill had given me hadn't been enough. It would never have been enough. The spike of desire had been overwhelming before he'd touched me, and it had completely taken over once he had. I'd needed his cock, needed to be filled, and that something that always snapped through me when we touched had crackled like lightning through my blood.

I scrambled off Lord Quill and grabbed the blanket that I'd clung to since the guys had rescued me, the urge to hide my shame twisting my insides.

"Hey," Lord Quill murmured as I pressed back

against the headboard and pulled the blanket up to my chin.

I needed to get ahold of myself. Be strong. A fae woman would never be embarrassed after sex. She'd be strong and sexy, languishing in the feel of her orgasm. But I was acting like a human and giving everything away.

He sat up but didn't try to draw closer, letting me keep the distance as if he knew approaching me would make me panic... which it would. Hell, I already was panicking.

"I—" My chest tightened and I fought to breathe. "I-I need you to leave."

The muscles in his jaw flexed and I could see the refusal on his lips.

"Please," I begged before he could say no.

"If I leave, West will enter." He glanced at the closed door leading to the sitting room before turning his stunning green gaze back to me. "Let me bathe you. Help you clean up first."

Right. Lord Quill had pulled rank on Sir West just to get me alone in the bedroom, and I had no doubt what Lord Quill said was true. Sir West would never leave me unattended. Even if Quill left the bedroom door open, Sir West would stand in the doorway and watch me. I wouldn't get the moment I needed to pull myself together.

The panic rose to my throat, turning my breaths into sharp gasps.

"Hey hey hey," he cooed as he crawled to my side and opened his arms. "May I?"

I stared at him. He wanted to hold me? Only Ash had ever offered me comfort like that and it hurt my soul knowing Ash should have been the one I'd had sex with, not Quill.

Except Lord Quill had been generous and gentle. I'd felt safe letting him touch me and I knew I'd feel safe if I let him hold me now.

I just had to remember I couldn't let it go further than a little comfort and a little sex.

Father, I couldn't let it go further than that with Ash, either.

I. Was. Human.

And fae didn't have permanent relationships with humans. We couldn't bear their children and we lived a fraction of their lives. The mating marks ringing my neck and me appearing in the Garden when only fae could enter, were a mistake, and if I let things get emotionally complicated, Ash and Quill would be furious with me.

That, and my life wasn't my own. I lived on borrowed time. Eventually the men of the Black Tower would learn the truth and I'd have to face the consequences.

"I know I'll never be your mate, but let me take care of you for now," he said.

I bowed my head. Lord Quill taking care of me was a much better choice than Sir West staring at me. "All right."

He scooped me from the bed, blanket and all, and carried me across the lavish bedroom and into a bathing room that was more opulent than anything I'd ever seen before.

The centerpiece was a stone tub sunk into the floor large enough to hold five or six people. Water, decorated with white and pink glowing flowers, filled it almost to the edge, and the air was thick with a warm mist, making me realize, now that the spike of desire had past, that I was cold.

Double doors at the back of the room stood open, revealing a breathtaking view of the lights from the other rooms in the tree-castle that made up the Divine Residence. I couldn't see into any of the other rooms — they were too far away — so I had no fear that someone could stand on their balcony and watch me bathe.

Lord Quill set me down on the edge of the tub and, still clutching the blanket to my front, I dipped my toes into the hot water. A warm shiver rolled through me, drawing a sigh, and I let my foot and calf sink into the heated depths.

"Don't get in yet," he said as he moved to an intricately carved set of shelves and gathered towels, a soft cloth, and fancy glass bottles. "I want to wash you first."

"Right. Need to wash off—" My face burned and I gestured to my crotch where Quill was slowly leaking from me.

He chuckled, the sound soft and sensual, even as a hint of sadness crept into his gaze. "If I were an animal shifter, I'd be offended at the suggestion to wash me off you."

"Oh, I—"

The image of Lord Rider furious that I'd wash him from me and ready to cover me again in his seed sent a shiver of desire rushing through me.

I quickly shoved that thought aside, praying that it had come from my desire spike and not something I actually wanted.

Lord Quill set the towel on a stone bench a few feet away and knelt beside me with the cloth and glass bottles. "You deserve to be worshiped. Let me worship you."

I nodded, my chest aching with how tight it was.

This handsome fae prince was going to shatter me. If I'd thought Ash had ruined me for having sex with any other man, Lord Quill was going to ruin me for everyone else.

He gently drew the blanket out of my grip then urged me to stand and helped me peel off my dress. A tremble shook my legs, and I clamped an arm across my breasts and a hand over my mound as my face heated with embarrassment. I'd only ever been naked in front of Ash, and it had been so dark — and my desire had been so strong — I hadn't cared.

But here, the soft fae light exposed everything and I couldn't bear for Quill to look at me.

Father, I was an idiot. I'd agreed to let him wash me. I *knew* that involved getting naked, but I hadn't realized how vulnerable I'd feel.

"You're so beautiful." He took one of the cloths, dipped it into the warm water in the tub, added a drop of something from one of the bottles, and began to gently wash my shoulders and back.

He didn't try to move my arms and kept the cloth in a safe, respectful location. I closed my eyes, focusing on the sensation of the warm water and the gentle pressure of his hands.

He wasn't going to hurt me. He'd saved me from Wells and Crane and those other men, and he'd stood up to Sir West to ensure I had privacy when we'd made love. He thought I was a fae woman and he wanted to comfort me.

In this moment, I could trust him.

I released a ragged breath and leaned into his touch, letting him ease the tension in my body. He worked his way down my right arm to my elbow then followed my forearm across my chest where he gently tugged on my wrist. I let him pull my arm away, and he moved the cloth with my arm instead of focusing on my chest. He did the same with my other arm, keeping his movements respectful.

Little snaps of attraction danced over my skin, and a sensual, slow heat unfurled inside me, but it wasn't the desperate need I'd felt from my mating marks. This was soft, tender. It had the potential to turn blistering, but Lord Quill didn't push for it and neither did I.

I needed time to feel safe and to work my head and heart around everything that had happened. I needed to cry out my grief and frustration and heartache. I needed to scream at the injustice of Sawyer being sent to the Gray, of Mikel and Durand and Wells and Crane thinking I could be their plaything. I needed— I needed—

"That's it," Lord Quill murmured as he trailed the cloth over my already damp cheeks. "I've got you."

My breath hitched and more tears leaked from my eyes.

Come on, Sage. Be strong.

But I couldn't stop the tears or the hiccupping gasps that shook my body.

Lord Quill wrapped his arms around me and I sagged to the floor, sobbing. He followed me down, holding me tight, and murmured something over and over again.

But I couldn't focus on his words.

I could only feel.

And I felt like I was breaking into a million jagged pieces.

I'd cried in Ash's arms, too, but that was over the horror of everything that had happened. Now I cried in Lord Quill's arms for everything I couldn't have.

CHAPTER 25

Ash

I stood at the entrance to the Sacred Grove, leaning on the wall beside the stone-tree arch that announced the beginning of its sacred passages, fighting to stay calm.

I didn't want to stand there waiting for Talon or the magister who Quill had contacted to free Sage from the artifact keeping her trapped in the Garden. I wanted to get back into the sacred pool's chamber and find evidence that pointed to everyone who was involved in attacking Sage.

But waiting here was just as important. If the High Priestess kept Talon, the magister wouldn't know Sage was in the Divine Residence and the night's trauma would be drawn out, something my soul screamed was unacceptable.

I clenched and unclenched my hands, my muscles twitching, desperate for movement.

Shadow shit! Stay calm.

If Lark couldn't get Rider's wolf to calm down, I was going to have to step up.

Goddess, please, let Lark calm Rider's wolf. When we'd left Phoenix's office, he was on the verge of losing it... Hell, he'd been on the verge of losing it the minute we'd stepped into the sacred pool's chamber and saw Sage hanging in the waterfall.

If the novices had pushed him to the edge, seeing what Wells, Crane, and those other men were doing to Red had thrown him over, and now I could only pray Lark could bring him back. We needed him. He was our leader. He'd always been our leader even before he'd become the Lord Commander of the Black Guard and we'd become his captains.

I knew he didn't think he was a very good leader. He didn't do *feelings* like Quill could, he couldn't break tensions with a quip like Talon, and he claimed he didn't understand complex motivations and subtext like me. He said he was too straightforward for that, and in a way he was. But he also understood his weaknesses, utilized the strengths of those around him, and encouraged a camaraderie among the guardsmen that the previous Lord Commander hadn't been able to.

And that thought only made me worry more about everything else going on. The novices this year were a disaster and adding in the attack on Sage — and how none of us were going to let it go, despite the High Priestess's warning — we were going to be wearing ourselves thin.

Sure, I was used to juggling multiple urgent matters at once. That was just the life of a spy, but Rider, Talon, and Quill weren't used to that level of chaos.

Lark might help Rider, but that still left Talon, who could barely control his shadow, and Quill, who was currently holding it together, but now that court was involved, he was dealing with his mother's machinations.

I jerked away from the wall and started pacing, unable to stay still any longer.

The situation with Sage complicated everything further. My connection to her was too strong, and it was clear the other guys were attracted to her as well, even if they didn't want to be. And now the High Priestess was involved. This wasn't going to end well.

A swirl of black smoke manifested a few feet away, coalescing into Talon's form. The black smoke thickened, turning into his shadow, and lashed out around his body sending a wave of desperate need crashing over me.

My cocked hardened and I bit back a moan. Every aching need I'd felt while bringing Sage relief from her mating marks earlier that night slammed through me a hundred times stronger, and the urge to find her, bury myself in her slick heat, screamed inside me.

Then the shadow rushed back into him, making him gasp and stagger forward.

"Fuck." He caught his balance and his gaze jerked around as if looking for witnesses before landing on me.

"We're alone," I assured him, my cock still hard and aching.

"And the magister?"

"Hasn't shown up yet."

"I hope this means he'll have everything he needs to release the new arrival and this won't get drawn out."

"She has a name," I snapped, unable to stop myself even though I knew not calling Sage by her name was a self-defense mechanism for him.

Out of all of us, he was the one who couldn't get close to her even if he wanted to. He couldn't risk her finding out about his shadow.

"What did the High Priestess say?"

He shot me a grim look. "Nothing good."

I waited for him to continue but he didn't, which made my chest tighten.

I wanted to know what they had talked about, especially if it had something to do with Sage — because anything to do with Sage and the High Priestess meant I had to protect Sage. But I couldn't push him. He'd tell me if it was important. I had to trust that.

Still, my mind whirled with all the possibilities. The High Priestess wasn't interested in Talon as a prospective mate for herself. She already had all of hers. But that didn't mean she wouldn't try to use him for something else. She loved toying with people, playing her games, and it looked like Sage was now her new favorite toy.

And standing here stewing wasn't going to help anything.

"I told Rider I'd do another check of the sacred pool," I said, and I glanced at the sky.

It was less than an hour until dawn, and I was going to have to get back to the Black Tower soon. Sure, it was a lieu day, but Mikel and the others were eager to get to Lehyrst. And I needed to stick with them to maintain my cover.

Thankfully, Rider had restricted Sawyer from leaving the Gray so there wasn't a chance of running into him, and it had sounded like everyone was going to treat him like a ghost from now on, but still, anything could happen.

"We'll meet, first thing, like usual tomorrow—" Talon followed my gaze upward. "Tonight."

He didn't add that first thing was our only option because the others were soon going to be in the Divine Residence to protect Sage and I couldn't follow, but I could hear the unspoken words hanging in the air between us.

All because the High Priestess liked to play games.

"Right." I marched through the archway into the Grove and headed toward the sacred pool.

I'd be more useful, be able to share right away what I learned from examining the pool if it weren't for the High Priestess and her cruel nature.

My thoughts leaped to Sage kneeling before Her Brilliance, her body curled tight even though her size no longer mattered — she'd already been spotted by the predator and trying to hide was useless.

The High Priestess was cruel to have dragged Sage in front of the court, and it was obvious how much all the attention had scared her.

It was bad enough Sage was an unmated woman, but then the High Priestess had to draw attention to Sage's magic, which just made all the unmated men at court even more interested in her.

I kicked a small stone off the path, watching it skitter into the vines. The High Priestess had the ability to sense someone's magical potential, and she would have dismissed Sage early if Sage's spark wasn't bright, not played out the whole game by asking about Sages family or by spirit linking her to West.

But no, she'd confirmed Sage's spark was bright, making her an ideal mate, drawing even more attention.

The memory of all those hungry gazes fixed on Sage made me want to scream.

Sage was soft and shy and sweet. The attack had already shaken her to her core, and then to be thrust into the spotlight like that...

Goddess be damned! We still didn't know enough about who was behind the attack. And now Sage had earned the High Priestess's attention.

For a moment I wondered if the High Priestess had something to do with Sage's attack.

Somehow the High Priestess knew almost right away about it and had summoned us. Although the more likely reason for the High Priestess being aware of the attack was because of her system of spies within the Garden.

Even I didn't know who all of them were.

Still, I couldn't shake the uneasy feeling as I continued down the winding paths toward the sacred pool. It could explain why the High Priestess had forced a soul link on Sage, binding her to an unmated, male stranger.

At least Quill was with her, even if I wish it was me.

Of course, once her shock wore off, she would undoubtedly be horrified by me. Maybe it was best that I was banned from entering the Divine Residence. My heart wouldn't be able to take it if she outright rejected me.

Except what if she didn't?

CHAPTER 26
Ash

I FOLLOWED the dimly lit winding path to the sacred pool's chamber but stopped short at the far end before reaching it. A knight stood guard at the entrance and another two headed down the path toward me carrying a stretcher with the body of one of Sage's attackers.

Damn it. The Order had already taken control of the chamber, and while I could change my spirit clothes so I wore the knights' uniform, I couldn't change my physical appearance in the Garden. My spirit form was stuck and even if my scarred face wasn't a giveaway that I wasn't a knight, my short hair would be, since all knights of the Order had to keep their hair a traditional length.

I wouldn't be able to search the pool for more clues

about the attackers who got away. Goddess. I was utterly useless.

Everything within me screamed I needed to protect Sage. Scouring the area where Sage had been attacked was the only useful thing I could do for her since I'd been useless in the throne room.

The knights carrying the stretcher drew closer, and I stepped back into the shadows and let my hair fall forward, veiling my face. I didn't recognize either of them, and I could only pray they were actually taking the corpse to the north wing to search for evidence and not some ditch outside of the Garden where no one would be able to find the body.

For a moment I considered following them, but if there was serious corruption within the Order, I doubt they'd make it obvious by not following procedure. No, once inside the Order's private wing, as much or as little of the investigation could be conducted and no one would be the wiser. Following the grunts carrying the corpses wouldn't get me anywhere.

But I also couldn't gather more information in the chamber. Which left me with what?

I wasn't sure what my next move was… if I even *had* a next move.

"Skulking in the shadows like usual," an all-too-familiar voice said from down the passage behind me.

Swell. Yarrow. The Order's most acclaimed investigator, and my older cousin.

I forced myself to keep my posture relaxed and turned to face him. He swept his magic-enhanced gaze over me, starting at my feet and finishing at my face. His magical ability to improve his vision wasn't particularly powerful, but combined with his quick intellect, it made him an effective investigator. And he took pleasure in reminding me he was the pride of the family while I was their greatest disappointment.

A hint of wicked mirth joined his sour expression, and for the millionth time since I was punished for it when we were children, I resisted the urge to strangle him.

"Phoenix assigned you the investigation," I forced out.

"Of course he did. I'm the best." The man was arrogant, self-important, utterly lacking in compassion, and unmated. He'd no doubt attempt to exploit his role to get close to Sage.

Hell, he probably saw this as his Goddess-given reward as a chance to court the newest arrival.

I could just see the fantasy in his head. He'd claim he apprehended all her attackers — whether he did or not — and Sage would swoon into mating him.

Except Sage would see right through him, and I didn't want to think what he'd do when she damaged his fragile ego.

"Her Brilliance has taken an interest in the new arrival, so I suggest you scurry back to the Gray."

I opened my mouth to tell him the new arrival had a name, but he cut me off.

"Do you actually think you're going to help?" He threw his head back and released a mocking laugh, loud enough to draw the attention of the knight guarding the entrance of the sacred pool. "That's adorable. You think if you step out of the shadows she won't scream with horror?"

She hadn't before... but that was just shock.

My throat tightened and I struggled to keep my expression empty. Yarrow wanted me to react so he could arrest me for interfering with his investigation.

Except I could already see it. The look of horror on her face, her trembling and frozen form. And the flinch. The same flinch all the others made when I took a single step closer.

The flinch that would shatter my soul.

"You did, didn't you?" His expression turned to fake pity. "Why do you even bother coming to the Garden? You know only beautiful people belong here? Actual candidates for providing the realm with the next generation. Not..." He gestured at my face, his lips curled in disgust. "Not whatever you are."

I clenched my jaw and his gaze jumped straight to the flexing muscles.

Shit. If I gave in to anger, I'd hand him the exact response he was fishing for and give him reason to report me to the Order. If the whim struck him, he could have me banned from most of the Garden and then I wouldn't be able to protect Sage at all.

I forced my jaw to relax and lowered my gaze, letting my hair fall forward to shield more of my face. "You're right. I don't belong here."

"Good. Now run along," Yarrow chuckled, his tone grating. "The real men have work to do."

I glanced back at the entrance to the sacred pool to take note of the man standing guard and released a resigned sigh before leaving Yarrow and his smirk. If the knight guarding the entrance didn't know me, I might be able to get him to talk about Yarrow's investigation.

Without a doubt, the Garden was already alive with gossip, but most of it would just be speculation, and while I could listen to it all, the best sources for information were the knight guarding the entrance, any knights inside the sacred pool's chamber, and Yarrow himself.

And while I could manipulate Yarrow into bragging about what he learned, the emotional toll was always high. It was better to save that for last and see what the knights working under him knew first.

Hell, it was better to break into Yarrow's office and riffle through his files.

But if nothing came out of it, I'd put up with Yarrow's demeaning attitude and cruel words. I'd do whatever it took to ensure Red was safe.

CHAPTER 27
Sage

LORD QUILL HUGGED me until my eyes were sore and dry and I was exhausted emotionally, physically, and mentally. Then he cradled me in his arms and sank into the tub.

I curled into him, unable to fight my need to be held, and let the hot water lull me into a hazy, numb state. I let all thought and emotion melt away. I focused only on the warmth relaxing my aching, bruised body and the sure, steady rhythm of Lord Quill's heart beating beneath my ear.

I wasn't sure how long he held me. It could have been minutes or hours. I didn't care. It was the time I needed to just be, where I wasn't the new arrival, Sawyer Herstind, a human, a fae, a woman, turned on, or anything else. I was just me.

The hazy numbness melted into the warmth of

Quill's embrace and the water, and I felt for the first time in a long time that I could breathe. My fate and everything that had happened still hung around me. I wasn't miraculously safe in the Garden or the Black Tower, and the vision I saw of my death still haunted me, but I refused to wallow in fear.

Fear wouldn't get me anywhere and it wouldn't protect Sawyer.

And Sawyer was my purpose.

I knew taking his place in the Black Guard would endanger my life and had decided in an instant that it was worth it. I still believed that.

Which meant I had to be brave and strong and face the consequences of my actions... even if half the things I was struggling with weren't because of something I'd done.

Sure, it wasn't fair. But life wasn't fair. If it were fair, my parents and my middle brother would still be alive.

At the moment, I couldn't control waking in the Garden, but I could choose how I reacted, and given that I was soul linked to Sir West, my reaction needed to be as bland and boring as possible.

A loud knock on the bedroom door startled me, and Lord Quill's grip around me tightened.

"Magister Zinnia has arrived," Sir West called through the closed door.

"Do you want to see her?" Lord Quill asked, his voice low.

"Yes." If everyone was going to continue believing I was fae, I needed answers. And since Zinnia knew I grew up in the human realm, she'd be able to help.

"Lady Sage will receive her in a moment," Quill called back.

He eased me off his lap onto the submerged bench and captured my gaze with his startling green eyes. "You don't have to talk to her if you don't want to."

"I—" I didn't know what to say. I couldn't tell him I needed to talk with her about how to be a fae woman... would I even be able to talk with her alone?

It had been difficult enough for Lord Quill to get Sir West to stay in the sitting room and close the door. What were the chances both of the men would leave me and Zinnia alone?

"I'd like to discuss my condition." Maybe that would give us some privacy.

"Of course." Lord Quill's gaze dipped to my magic-less mating marks. "There should be a robe in the wardrobe."

He stood, sending the water rushing around his body and drawing my attention to his muscular chest and abs and his semi-hard cock.

Heat burned my cheeks at seeing him naked as well as remembering how I'd jumped him, and I wrenched around to stare at the wall. The sudden movement sent pain rushing through my abused body, and I bit back a groan.

"Let me help you stand," he said, offering me his hand and thankfully not commenting on my embarrassment or the fact that I looked away from his naked form.

I took it and rose on shaky legs. It was the right call not letting Zinnia completely heal me, but boy was I going to hurt when I returned to my body... and I was not going to think about how time was ticking away, drawing closer and closer to dawn and perhaps my inevitable discovery in the Black Tower.

Quill helped me climb out of the tub and handed me a large, fluffy towel. He didn't offer to help dry me, as if he knew that would be too much for me, and he didn't encourage me to face him, letting me keep my back to him.

It was silly to be embarrassed about him seeing me naked. He already had, and he had plenty of time to stare at me while I'd cuddled in his embrace and floated in that hazy numbness, but I couldn't help myself. I'd only ever been naked with Ash once, and that wasn't enough to get over years of being told I needed to stay covered.

A flash of color from the corner of my eye caught my attention, and Lord Quill was instantly dressed. He hadn't even dried off with a towel and didn't look damp.

Of course if I could change my spirit clothes, I'd

probably be able to imagine myself dry and wearing a heavy robe that covered everything.

He wore a green and gold tunic that looked fancier than the ones I'd seen him wear before. The color made his emerald eyes shimmer and for a moment I was at risk of falling into his gaze again. But before I could get caught in whatever magic it was that drew me to him, he strode into the bedroom to a large, intricately carved wardrobe, and pulled out a silky, red robe.

He draped it over my shoulders and for a moment it looked like he wanted to say something, but he jerked away instead and headed to the closed bedroom door.

I secured the robe, making sure it covered all of my sleeping mating marks, and he opened the door. Sir West stepped inside, forcing Lord Quill to take a step back, and Sir West's sapphire gaze snapped to me in the bathing room's entrance as if he knew exactly where I was... and with the spirit link, I guess he did.

A shudder teased down my spine, and I tensed, refusing to let it show. I didn't want anyone knowing where I was at all times and certainly not this monstrous knight who I didn't know and didn't trust.

"I wish to speak with Sage about her condition," Zinnia said from the sitting room. "West, you can wait out here."

Sir West's attention jerked to the sitting room and

the muscles in his jaw clenched. For a moment, I feared he'd refuse Zinnia. He didn't look any angrier than he had when he'd first been assigned to guard me, but given that "grim" seemed to be his only expression, I wasn't sure if I'd know if he was angry or not.

Lord Quill telling him to wait in the sitting room while he helped relieve the pressure from the mating marks had to have pissed him off. Now he was being told to wait in the sitting room again.

I had no doubt Zinnia was going to shut the door between us so we could talk. And if she wasn't, I was.

It was bad enough Zinnia thought I was a fae slave in the human realm. I couldn't afford for Sir West to overhear that and for him to tell the High Priestess.

"Magister," Sir West rumbled and he stormed back into the sitting room.

Zinnia took his place in the doorway. "You, too, Quill."

The Captain of the White Tower turned to me, his gaze searching mine, the question in his eyes clear. Did I want him to stay?

"It's all right."

"I'll just be on the other side of the door," he said as he stepped past Zinnia.

She closed the door behind him and gestured to a small seating area by the window.

It was more of a nook with a cushioned window seat covered with soft pillows, and a highbacked, cushioned chair than a conversation area, but it was as far away from the bedroom as we could get without going into the bathing room.

I sat on the window seat and brushed my fingers through the leaves and flowers trailing over the windowsill, watching the delicate white and pink light dance under my touch.

Zinnia drew the chair as close to the window seat as possible before leaning back against its plush cushions.

"How are you holding up?" she asked, her voice low.

"Better. Steadier." Grateful she didn't ask why I was alone in the bedroom with Lord Quill while Sir West had been banished to the sitting room.

Although she'd probably already figured everything out. Fae were more open about sex than humans and she'd warned me that I'd experience spikes of desire while I waited for the magic that put my mating marks to sleep to settle.

And that wasn't the point of this conversation. I needed to stay focused and learn about all the things I didn't know.

"Good. Give me your hand so I can assess your injuries and mating marks."

"Nothing has changed." I peeled back the neck of my robe just enough to show her my magicless marks. As for my injuries, my cheek still hurt, so I assumed the bruise was forming nicely and would be a brilliant purple by morning.

She tsked and held out her hand. "Humor me."

Fine. I placed my hand in hers, but instead of the warmth of her magic sinking beneath my skin, she tightened her grip and met my gaze.

"I can get you out of the human realm and protect that child."

I wrenched my hand out of hers, my pulse suddenly racing. "I can't leave."

"Not even if I assure you there'll be no repercussions for you, and that the child will be safe and cared for?" A strange expression flitted across Zinnia's face, but it was so fast I wasn't sure what it meant.

"No. I told you."

She didn't know what she was saying, and she certainly didn't know that she couldn't rescue me from the human realm because I was actually a human. It was the fae realm where I didn't belong.

"It's complicated." I'd already explained that to her.

I'd thought when I said that I'd tell her the minute I could leave I would that she'd believed me, but I also couldn't deny how terrible the situation looked from her perspective.

If I were in her position, I'd want to rescue the abused woman and child, and I'd be willing to risk the wrath of an entire nation to do so.

Of course, I already was risking more than one

nation's wrath. Taking Sawyer's place in the Black Guard subverted the lottery and the punishment would be severe.

"I know how it looks. But you have to trust me. It won't be forever. I can handle the human realm." I grabbed her hand, capturing it between both of my palms, and met her gaze. "I don't know if I can handle the fae realm. I don't know how to behave or what to be wary of."

It would be best if I could figure out how to stop manifesting in the Garden when I went to sleep, and I could only pray that would stop happening now that Zinnia had removed the magic from my mating marks.

But I couldn't count on that.

I had to assume I was always going to end up in the Garden and plan accordingly. And if my nightly visits stopped, I'd consider that a happy accident.

Even if a small part of me wept at the thought.

A part I didn't want to look too closely at.

No, what I needed was to focus on the most immediate problems, and the biggest one — pun absolutely intended — was Sir West and the spirit link that the High Priestess had forced on us.

I huffed in frustration. It was ridiculous that the men who'd attacked me and escaped, who could still be plotting to kidnap me again and force me to bond with them, were now my second biggest problem.

CHAPTER 28
Sage

"I'D SAY you don't have to be wary of anyone," Zinnia said, "but after the audience with Her Brilliance, I have to say you should be wary of *everyone*."

Swell. That was my original assumption. I'd just hoped I'd been wrong.

"And that includes Sir West?" I asked, lowering my voice even more. I really didn't want him to overhear our conversation. "How serious is the soul link?"

"It's something only the High Priestess can create and is usually reserved for Her Brilliance's protection and those who are precious to her."

Or someone who made an interesting toy. If I hadn't caught her attention — or if she didn't have some other, deeper plot — Sir West and I wouldn't have been stuck together. I doubted it had anything to do with my magic like she'd suggested.

Sure, seeing into the future was powerful. But I couldn't control it, and up until a few days ago, all I'd gotten were feelings that something bad was going to happen. I hadn't actually *seen* anything until Sawyer had been summoned to the Gray, and all I'd seen or sensed were deaths. Ones I could only pray I could prevent.

My thoughts whirled and my chest tightened. Maybe I was wrong. Maybe the High Priestess did know I could see the future, knew my abilities were growing, and wanted to use me.

Hell, I was betting my life on the fact that I could change what I'd seen, something I hadn't been able to do before I'd started having visions.

It was foolish to think I couldn't learn to control my ability or that I wouldn't be able to see other things, things that didn't involve people dying.

Which maybe made me an extremely valuable resource.

Shit. Nothing was guaranteed, and if anyone knew more about my ability it would be the High Priestess. And just because the High Priestess said Sir West and I would only be linked until I bonded all my mates didn't mean she wouldn't change her mind and keep me linked to him as a way to control me.

Father! I'd already fallen into her trap and there wasn't any way to escape.

"Sage." Zinnia leaned closer, concern etching her face. "It'll be all right."

"Can Her Brilliance tell what a person's magic is?" I whispered.

"No. She can only tell how powerful it might become."

So she didn't know the truth. I could still escape if I convinced her I had a powerful but useless— maybe useless wasn't the word. Boring. I needed to convince her I had a powerful but boring magic.

Jeez, what magic could even be considered boring? All magic was incredible.

"Is your magic dangerous?"

If I could control what I saw and I could foresee things other than death... then yeah, in the wrong hands it could be very dangerous.

"Have you told anyone?" Zinnia asked without waiting for me to confirm if my magic was dangerous or not.

"No."

"Don't. And don't tell me. A secret is safest if only one person knows."

I couldn't disagree with her, but if I couldn't control my visions, there was a chance I could have one in the Garden and the monster to whom I was soul linked would notice.

My pulse lurched as a new horrible thought struck

me. "Can Sir West feel what I'm feeling? Can he see through my eyes? How linked are our souls?"

"He can only feel if you're in extreme distress and he can't see through your eyes. The strong emotions aside, all it does is make you hyperaware of where the other person is," Zinnia said. "Can you sense West in the sitting room?"

I close my eyes to concentrate on Sir West. I hadn't noticed him before, but I'd been distracted, first by my overwhelming desire and then by the comforting numbness.

"You shouldn't have to concentrate," Zinnia interrupted before I could get started. "If Her Brilliance had set up the link for you to be aware of Sir West, you'd know it. He'd be a buzzing presence in your mind that you wouldn't be able to fully ignore."

No wonder Sir West had looked grim when he'd climbed the stairs to the High Priestess's throne. He had to have known what Her Brilliance was going to do.

Which meant maybe he was just as much of a victim in the High Priestess's game as I was.

Maybe being stuck with him wouldn't be so bad. Maybe I could trust him.

The memory of his grim expression and the fact that he had every intention of watching me while I went to the bathroom flashed through my mind's eye.

And maybe I was just grasping at desperate hope and had to accept the truth that Sir West wasn't an ally.

"Tell me about Sir West." Knowledge was power and the slightest detail could protect me.

"I can't tell you much," she said. "I don't know much. He's a formidable knight but keeps to himself, even among the other knights."

"What about family? Friends?" There had to be something.

"His mother and all but one of his fathers were killed during a magical experiment." Zinnia's gaze drifted out the window as if she couldn't look me in the eyes for her next words. "His remaining father is in a special house for men who've lost bonded mates. Most recover from a broken bond, but not all."

"What does that mean?"

Zinnia's attention jumped to me, her expression startled before shifting to realization.

"Right. You don't know anything about your birth realm," she said. "It's traumatic losing a bonded mate and it can affect someone's mind. I'm not familiar with West's father. I can heal spirit and body but not soul. But I know of the residence where he's being cared for, and they only take the most serious cases."

Which meant Sir West was alone. Like I was.

"You also need to know what it means for the High Priestess to have invited you to her court," Zinnia added. "You should expect all of Her Brilliance's courtiers, including those who weren't in the throne room during your audience, to want to court you."

Of course they would, I thought glumly.

"But, unlike in the human realm, you can tell a fae man what you want, what you think, and for him to leave you alone."

Except I was sure I had to at least give him a chance before I told him to go away.

The thought twisted my stomach. I'd already told Wells and Crane to leave me alone and that had ended in disaster.

"I know it's going to be difficult. I've heard how women in the human realm are expected to behave, and I know the men are stricter with slaves." Zinnia grabbed my hands in hers. "But I've seen your strength. I know you can handle this and I'll teach you what I can."

As we continued to talk, the sky outside the window grew lighter and lighter with hues of pink and gold spilling across the horizon. Zinnia's voice was soothing, her information helpful, but with each passing moment the knot of anxiety twisted tighter in my stomach.

Dawn in the Garden meant dawn in the Gray, and with every flicker of golden light through the softly swaying leaves and branches, the urgent reality of my situation loomed larger.

My room in the Black Tower didn't have a lock, and anyone could walk in on me and discover my secret.

A sharp knock yanked me from my spiraling thoughts, and the bedroom door cracked open.

"Magister Aster has arrived to remove the bracelet," Lord Quill said.

My churning unease grew. The magister could save me, but without a doubt, he'd need to get close to me and use his magic to remove the bracelet. Zinnia hadn't realized I was human — or she hadn't said anything — when she'd used her magic to heal me, but there was no guarantee Magister Aster wouldn't learn the truth.

"He's the best in the White Tower with unusual magics," Zinnia said as she stood. "We'll return your spirit to your body before your human master knows you've been gone."

I glanced back out the window at the rising sun.

"I'm sure of it," Zinnia assured me.

I could only pray that was true.

CHAPTER 29
Sage

ZINNIA and I crossed the bedroom, and when we reached the door, Lord Quill stepped back into the sitting room to let us pass, while Sir West — who stood against the wall beside the door — straightened and loomed over me.

I squared my shoulders, refusing to cower under his dower expression and brilliant sapphire gaze. Zinnia had assured me Sir West wouldn't punish me for being confident. He might have been assigned to protect me by the High Priestess, but unless it involved my safety, *I* was in charge.

Except I had no idea what Sir West would consider involving my safety or not. He'd already said he'd watch me and everything I did, and that I couldn't leave the tree-castle to be with Ash — at least not until my remaining attackers were apprehended.

What else could I ask for? Ash was the only one I wanted. I didn't want anyone or anything else.

Talon, along with a handsome fae man who looked as old as my stepfather, Edred, but was probably a couple hundred years old, stood at the entrance to the suite. The Captain of the Gold Tower's mesmerizing gaze locked with mine. He had a strange look in his eyes, an emotion I couldn't place and wasn't sure I wanted to. And even with that strange look, heat crept across my cheeks.

Father, he was so beautiful, and it didn't matter that Zinnia had put my mating marks to sleep. I was still drawn to him, drawn to the memory of his allure — that aching, desperate need created by the shadow trapped within him.

His gaze drifted down my neck and the heat of desire quickly shifted to embarrassment.

The look in his eyes had to be veiled pity and disgust. But because I was now the High Priestess's toy, he couldn't show how he really felt. I'd cowered in the throne room. I'd wanted to hide it, but I was sure anyone looking at me had known how scared I'd been.

Sure, he'd been nice and seemed concerned, but he was here because he'd needed to escort the magister to my room, not because he was as attracted to me as I was to him. Nothing I'd done between our first meeting and now could have changed his mind about risking his secret with a woman he didn't know.

And why did that bother me? It shouldn't have. I wasn't interested in him. I didn't trust him. I didn't want to be in the Garden with his or anyone else's attention.

Except Ash's.

Nausea churned in my stomach.

No. Not even Ash's. I had to remember my purpose.

"Magister Aster," Zinnia said, and I wrenched my attention from Talon to the older fae.

He wore robes like Zinnia did, but instead of pale blue, his were pale yellow, with panels of golden embroidery down the front. His long, silver-blue hair hung to his waist and was held back with thin braids at either temple in a hair style similar to Talon's, and he wore ruby earrings in his delicately pointed ears that matched his ruby eyes.

"Magister Zinnia," Aster said with a dip of his head.

"This is my patient, Lady Sage." Zinnia led me to one of the soft couches in the middle of the sitting room and we sat.

"My lady." Magister Aster dipped his head toward me as well, then strode across the sitting room to stand in front of me. "A chair, if you please," he said without looking away from me.

"Of course, magister," Quill said, and he grabbed one of the highbacked, wooden chairs at the dining table and placed it beside the magister.

Aster sat, and in four long strides Sir West was at the magister's side with his arms crossed.

"Ah, the guard dog," Aster muttered, his voice so quiet I had to strain to hear it. "I'm not here to harm her."

Sir West didn't react, as if he hadn't heard the magister speak, and Aster rolled his eyes and turned back to me.

"Talon explained your spirit is being held here by an artifact. A bracelet," he said. "May I see it?"

My pulse skipped a beat. Here it was. The moment when Magister Aster could discover I was a human while also freeing me from the Garden.

Please let the longest night of my life be over soon.

I reached to push up my sleeve, but Zinnia placed her hand on mine, stopping me.

"She's also affected by an unusual magic. You should look at that first. I'm sure her spirit will return to her body the moment you remove the bracelet."

Magister Aster frowned. "You're probably right. Let's look at this magic first." He glanced at Zinnia. "You say it's unusual?"

"I've never seen anything like it," Zinnia replied.

"May I?" he asked me, holding his hand out palm up.

I placed my hand in his, fighting to keep my expression calm, and his magic snapped over the back of my hand.

Where Zinnia's magic was warm and soothing, Aster's magic was sharp and biting.

It crawled painfully up my arm and into my chest, drawing a sharp gasp. Sir West, Lord Quill, and Talon all jerked forward a step.

"She's all right," Zinnia said, even as she met my gaze, her eyes asking for confirmation.

I nodded and bit down on the inside of my cheek to keep from making any more noise, even though I couldn't stop myself from flinching every time his magic bit into me.

Aster hummed and frowned and mumbled about how the magic was strange as his fingers twitched against mine. He didn't react to my flinches as if he were completely oblivious to my pain despite sitting right in front of me.

After a too-long painful moment he turned to Zinnia. "Look at it with me. I'd like your thoughts."

"Of course." She took my free hand and her warm soothing magic seeped under my skin.

The two powers clashed, and a sudden sharp snap shot through my chest. I yelped and Sir West grabbed Aster.

My pulse lurched. He was going to pull the magister away, and I'd have to do this all over again.

"Don't you dare. I'm only doing this once," I snarled at Sir West.

He glared back at me but thankfully released Aster without stopping the magister.

I didn't know how long Magister Aster and Zinnia examined the magic within me. I couldn't sense a foreign power coursing through my veins, but I didn't doubt Zinnia that it was there.

Finally, Aster and Zinnia withdrew their magic and let go of my hands. Shuddering with aftershocks, I sagged back against the couch and drew in deep breaths, fighting to steady myself.

"Are you all right?" Lord Quill asked as he dropped into a crouch beside Aster's chair.

He reached out as if he wanted to touch me, reassure me, but didn't finish the move, and his hand dropped to his knee instead.

It hurt to think he didn't want to touch me, and yet I understood his hesitation. We'd had sex, but that didn't mean there was anything between us.

Sure, we shared an attraction, but that didn't necessarily mean anything, either. Sex and attraction didn't mean the same things in the fae culture as it did in the human one.

"The magic isn't as strong as it was when I first examined it," Zinnia said, not reacting to the moment Lord Quill and I were sharing. "I think it's fading."

"That was my assumption as well," Aster added. "It's unlike any magic I've come across but it doesn't look like it's anchored to anything, and I believe it'll naturally dissipate."

Doesn't look.

Believe.

The words didn't inspire confidence. I didn't like the idea of them leaving the magic inside me. It had almost mate bonded me with Wells against my will.

"I agree," Zinnia said, destroying any hope that Zinnia would support me if I demanded Aster remove it.

Of course... *could* Magister Aster remove it?

I met Aster's ruby gaze, the question on the tip of my tongue, and his expression went blank.

From that look I knew I could ask, but he wouldn't answer me because he wasn't going to admit to something he couldn't do.

"Let me see the bracelet," he said, brushing off the moment between us.

I considered, just for a moment, saying something, making Sir West and the others aware that Magister Aster couldn't remove the magic, but that wouldn't help me. I still needed him to remove the bracelet. That, and I had no doubt he had powerful magic. It'd be foolish to make him an enemy.

I pushed up the sleeve of my robe and showed him the bracelet. Again he frowned and hummed.

"Can you remove it?" Talon asked.

"Look at this craftsmanship," Aster mumbled,

ignoring Talon. "The magical skill needed to craft something so exquisite..."

"Do you recognize it, magister?" Quill asked as he gingerly placed a hand on Aster's knee.

"Recognize it?" Aster blinked... and blinked again. Then his unfocused gaze landed on Quill. "I don't, but the Head of Artifacts at the White Tower might." His gaze drifted to the open balcony doors and the bright blue sky. "It's a beautiful piece. Powerful and rare."

Father! For the love of—!

"Rare isn't helpful," I snapped, unable to stop myself.

Quill flinched at my sudden outburst, and embarrassment heated my face, but I couldn't back down from this. The strange magic that had been affecting my marks, sure. I didn't feel any different and as far as I knew I wasn't in immediate danger.

But the bracelet could kill me.

"Can you remove it?" I demanded.

Aster tilted his head, the movement birdlike and disturbing. "I have no idea."

"You have—!"

No.

No no no.

I couldn't stay here. Not like this.

My attention jerked to Lord Quill and Talon. They were in the room with me. I knew they weren't in the Gray, but I had no idea where Lord Rider was. For all I knew he'd returned his spirit to his body and was going to wake me for another round of punishments.

"It'll be all right." Zinnia grabbed my hand and soothing magic swept into me.

One moment panic tightened my chest, the next I slouched on the couch, my thoughts muddled.

"What are you—?" I jerked my hand away and my panic rushed back in.

She could control my emotions, not just heal my spirit and physical forms, and I shuddered to think what could be done with a magic that powerful. Did I trust her because she was trustworthy or because she'd convinced me with her magic?

She gave an almost imperceptible shake of her head as hurt and begging filled her eyes. She was silently pleading with me to know that she hadn't influenced me.

Father, how I wanted to believe that.

But it didn't matter what I believed. I'd know soon enough if she betrayed my trust. She knew more about me and my situation than anyone else.

"Sage," Quill said, drawing my attention to him. "Magister Aster is a master of archaic and magical devices."

Which meant if Aster couldn't free me, no one could?

I didn't want to accept this man was my only hope.

"And it's a fascinating artifact," Aster added.

"Which you can study after you've gotten it off Lady Sage's wrist," Talon said.

Aster chuckled, somehow oblivious to my panic and the tension between me and... well, everyone in the room including him.

"So impatient," he hummed as he took the bracelet in both hands.

His sharp magic bit into me, slicing up my arm and making my eyes water. I clenched my jaw and fought to breathe through my nose, desperate to look like it didn't feel like Aster was sawing my arm off.

Black spots danced at the edge of my vision, and my pulse pounded faster. I was going to pass out.

Please, Father, don't let me pass out.

The spots swarmed larger, and my vision narrowed to the bracelet and the catch between Aster's hands.

A violent snap sliced across my chest and I jerked, but Aster held tight to the bracelet. With a sharp click, the latch released, my wrist slipped free, and I was falling backward.

CHAPTER 30

Quill

THE BRACELET SLIPPED from Sage's delicate wrist and she vanished, leaving only the crumpled silk robe fluttering down into the couch cushions. My chest tightened with a churning mix of relief, yearning, and regret. Relief that she was finally free to return to her body, but regret that she was beyond my ability to protect... like Sawyer's sister.

I shoved that thought as far back as I could, even though I knew it was going to keep haunting me. It had haunted me while I'd bathed and held her, and while I'd fought to sit on the couch in the sitting room while she talked with Zinnia.

Hell, everything about those women haunted me.

When I'd bathed Sage, I couldn't stop wondering if Sawyer's sister was bruised like Sage. Sawyer had said their father had hit them. Had his sister's bruises healed by now or did she have more?

Sawyer had claimed she was safe, but was she? Everyone had thought Sage had been safe but Wells and Crane had proven us wrong. And a human woman in the human realm couldn't possibly be safe.

The urge to find her twisted my insides, but so, too, did the urge to find Sage. Her trembling sobs when I'd washed her had shattered my heart. I'd never seen a fae woman so small and broken. If we hadn't saved her, she would have—

I didn't want to think what would have happened. She'd killed Wells out of sheer determination, but after hitting her head like she had, she wouldn't have been able to fend off the other men.

No, she would have continued to fight. She'd only shown me how much they'd hurt her because she'd felt safe... something I wanted to ensure Sawyer's sister felt.

Goddess, I was losing my mind.

I had to pull my shit together. I wasn't done. I still had to tell the others about Sage's mating marks, and we needed a plan to protect her from my mother — even if that meant murdering West and hiding his body. And planning wasn't going to happen while I was still in a room with West, Zinnia, and Aster.

Beside me, Aster stayed seated in the dining chair

clutching the bracelet, his red eyes bright with curiosity.

Swell.

I'd seen that look on a lot of magisters when they were focused on their work or had found something intriguing and knew if I didn't say something, he'd be lost in thought for hours.

"Magister Aster," I said, hoping just talking with him would catch his attention. "You'll ensure the bracelet is returned to the White Tower?"

He slowly turned his head and blinked at me. "Hmm? Oh, yes, yes." His gaze dropped back to the bracelet. "It's so interesting. The physical and magical craftsmanship is exquisite. The—"

I glanced at Talon as he came up beside me. He rolled his eyes and raised a silver eyebrow at me. Aster was brilliant, but he easily became lost in his work — like a lot of magisters in the White Tower did, actually.

"Aster," I insisted, my tone sharper than I wanted.

If the bracelet hadn't been a clue as to who'd been involved in Sage's attack, I wouldn't have cared. But even if the Order caught all the men who'd been in the sacred pool's chamber, that didn't mean everyone had been apprehended, and the bracelet could help us figure out who was left.

"It's essential the artifact is secured in the White Tower," I said. "You can study it after it's been cata-logued by the Head of Artifacts."

Aster wrenched his attention away from the bracelet and met my gaze. "You have my word."

He stood, slipped the artifact into a velvet-lined pouch hanging from his belt — as if to prove he could focus on something other than the bracelet — and headed to the door. But he was mumbling about it before the door to the suite had even closed.

"You'll want to follow up on that," Talon said. "Would hate for that evidence to go missing."

I hated that thought as well, but I couldn't confiscate the bracelet. I was in the Garden in my spirit form. The moment I left the Garden's boundaries, my spirit form would dissolve and the bracelet would fall to the ground where anyone could pick it up.

"I'll make sure it gets to the Head of Artifacts," Zinnia said as she stood.

"Wait." West stepped in front of her, stopping her from leaving the couch. "Tell me about Sage's condition first. How severe is her memory loss?"

"You know I can't discuss a patient's condition with you." Zinnia glanced at me and Talon. "Or any of you. But I'll say this. Don't expect her to behave the way you think she should."

Talon nodded. "Even without the memory loss, she's been traumatized and I have it on good authority that she's painfully shy."

West stiffened. "Whose authority?"

I studied his expression, but it didn't change so I

couldn't figure out what the tightening of his posture meant.

"As far as I know Ash and Rider are the only ones who've spent time with her," Talon said as West's gaze rose to meet mine.

"This was my first time saying more than a few words to her." And we hadn't really said much to each other this time as well... which was good, because I might have forgotten she wasn't Sawyer's sister and asked her for her name. "Ash has confirmed that she's avoided the courtyard after her initial arrival."

"And Rider told me she'd been using his name as a shield to avoid spending time with anyone," Talon added.

West's grim expression darkened, but again, I had no idea what that meant. Was he angry with Sage for using Rider's name to protect herself? Or had it reminded him of what had happened to her? Or did it piss him off that she was going to be slow bonding with her mates because she was shy?

If the latter was the case, he was going to be furious to learn her marks were asleep and she wouldn't be bonding with anyone anytime soon.

"I suggest the Order hurry their investigation," Zinnia said jabbing a finger into West's chest. "Captain Ash is important to her, and I doubt you'll be able to complete your duty without him."

Guess Zinnia also believed that Ash was Sage's first mate.

"If you'll excuse me," she said and she strode out of the suite.

West turned his glare back on me, reminding me that we were in his and Sage's suite. He had the spirit anchor on him, but would he risk leaving and having Sage manifest where he couldn't easily protect her?

"Well." I stood, met Talon's gaze, and jerked my chin toward the door indicating we should leave. "I'll see you tomorrow evening, Sir West."

"That's not necessary, Your Highness," West said, his voice a deep, emotionless rumble.

"And yet..." I left, not waiting for West to remind me there wasn't any point to me visiting Sage. He had to be thinking it. I had no magic. The Goddess would never bond us.

"And yet..." Talon chuckled as he followed me into the quiet hall and closed the door behind us. "Well played. Still," he said as he pulled me into a hug. "I'm sorry you had to become His Highness again."

I leaned into his embrace. Goddess, I loved the feel of his arms around me, loved how I felt safe and secure and supported. My chest tightened with churning emotions I needed to ignore. What I wanted and how I felt didn't matter at the moment. Only keeping Sawyer's sis— *Sage!* Only keeping *Sage* safe mattered.

"Not here," I whispered in his ear.

He drew back and met my gaze. I glanced at the door to Sage's suite and he nodded. We'd spent enough time working together that he understood I didn't want anyone overhearing our conversation and not that I didn't want him holding me.

We manifested our spirit forms at the entrance to the Sacred Grove and hurried to the now not-quite-so-secret conception suite where we'd brought Sage. It was still the most secure spot in the Garden.

"Do you know where Rider and Ash are?" I asked the minute the door closed behind us.

"Ash returned to the Black Tower to keep an eye on the novices, what with Sawyer threatening to murder Mikel and his group in their sleep." Talon rubbed his face, suddenly looking exhausted.

Shit. Had that only been yesterday?

It felt like a lifetime ago.

"It's also a lieu day, and all the novices are usually the first ones through the gate to Lehyrst," Talon added. "Ash can't afford to miss that if he wants to maintain his cover, and I should get going soon. It's my turn to monitor Lehyrst and make sure the novices don't make trouble."

I sagged onto the couch and stared at the magical fire in the hearth. The flames had burst to life when we'd entered, offering soft light and warmth, but it couldn't relax me. With Sage gone, with a moment to breathe and think, everything that had happened came crashing down.

Except I couldn't wallow or let my whirlwind thoughts and emotions whip through me. "I'm assuming, given that it's already full morning, that Rider returned to the Gray."

"That's my guess as well. Ash had said he went to talk with Lark to calm his wolf and that the sacred pool's chamber was swarming with Order knights." Talon sat on the couch beside me and pulled me back into his arms. "The Order's investigator is Yarrow, by the way."

"So we still have no idea if we can trust anyone in the Order."

Yarrow was an excellent investigator, and he wouldn't stop until he, personally, knew the truth. But he was devoutly dedicated to the Order, and if Lord Commander Phoenix told him to withhold any or all information, he would, and he wouldn't ask questions.

And that wasn't nearly as important as dealing with West.

"I know you don't want to be anywhere near her—" I started but Talon cut me off.

"You can't be with her at all times. I'm willing the share guard duty with you and Rider."

I pulled back, surprised. Talon had avoided all unmated women since being infected with his shadow because he couldn't afford to be bonded with anyone. He even had to be rude to get them to stay away.

"And you're all right with this? You can't be mean to her while you're with her." I doubted West would stand for it, and I couldn't bear the thought, either.

I'd held her while she cried and sat nearly comatose in the bath for almost an hour and then I watched her rebuild herself one breath at a time. It was slow and steady, a powerful determination that started as a faint glimmer in her eyes and carefully grew.

She was still shy — that much was obvious when Aster had showed up — and being trapped by the bracelet had still scared her, but I knew when we'd stepped out of the tub she'd regained the same strength she'd had when she'd killed Wells.

And I had to protect that spark.

"We have to be in the suite when she manifests tonight. Whatever Wells and Crane did, it messed with her marks and Zinnia had to put them asleep."

Talon's eyes flashed wide. "For how long?"

"She doesn't know. But my mother will lose her mind if she can't use Sage."

"West might lose his mind as well." Talon huffed. "I doubt your mother will remove the spirit link if Sage turns out to be a broken toy. She'll just forget about Sage and West and move on to the next game."

"Unless West is more valuable than he looks."

But he had to have a powerful magical ability for

him to be valuable enough for Her Brilliance to care that he was spirit linked to a woman who might never be bonded and never conceive children. My mother tossed me aside without a second thought, and I'd spend my entire childhood training to be a mate to a High Priestess.

"I'd have to confirm with Ash, but I think linking West to Sage was just part of her game." Talon stood and offered me his hand. "Let's get back to the Gray and talk to Rider. Here's hoping we can convince West it's in his best interest not to mention Sage's marks to your mother."

"Here's hoping Rider's wolf will stay calm enough for us to convince West," I said, taking his hand.

Rider was protective of women whether he was interested in them or not, and given how he'd reacted to Sage being attacked there was a chance he was actually interested.

CHAPTER 31

Sage

I JERKED, my eyes flying open as agony screamed through my body. Everything hurt. My face, my arms, my chest, my legs. Father, I was dying.

"Sawyer, open up!" an angry voice yelled, followed by banging on the wooden door to my room in the Black Tower. "Sawyer, we're coming in."

My pulse lurched.

Oh shit, oh shit, oh shit.

There wasn't a lock on my door. I had to get up. Were my breasts flattened or had the fabric binding them loosened while I slept? I needed to put my jerkin on. Get as covered as possible, and covering myself with my blankets would only make me look weak and make them ask more questions.

I scrambled off the bed. My body screamed in

protest and my legs gave out. I hit the floor with an *oomph* just as the door opened.

"Shadows!" Kit gasped as he strode the two steps to me and helped me sit on the edge of my bed. He glared over his shoulder at Payne. "I told you not to yell."

Payne returned his mate's glare. "He wasn't answering."

"And now you've scared the life out of him," Kit shot back before grabbing my chin and angling my face so he could look at my bruised cheek.

The handsome fae winced at what he saw, and before he could check out the rest of me, I crossed my arms over my breasts — realizing, thankfully! that I still wore my jerkin. I'd been so tired after running the trail, I hadn't changed out of my sweaty, grimy, vomit-smelling clothes. I'd just passed out.

At least I had that. I was disheveled and sore, but I didn't immediately look like a girl.

"Pretty sure Rider already scared the life out of him," Lewin said as he pushed Payne into the small room and entered himself.

Grefin leaned against the doorframe. "The runt is still alive. Can we get breakfast now? I'm starving."

"*You* can go get food," Payne said to Grefin before jerking his chin at me. "You, stand."

What? Was I in trouble?

I glanced at Kit. He looked... worried? Although his expression could be angry instead of worried. Was he also pissed that I'd threatened Mikel and his cronies?

Everyone had to have heard what had happened. It was the only explanation why Kit and his team had barged into my room. What I didn't know was if they were as angry as Rider had been.

"Sawyer," Payne growled. "Stand and show us how bad it is."

"How bad—?"

"Jeez guys. He finally gets a day to sleep in and you bang down his door." Grefin rolled his eyes. "We heard what Rider made you do. These three need to know if they have to carry you to Flint for healing or if a soak in a healing pool and walking it off will do."

Oh.

"Really. I'm fine." I rose on shaky legs and tried not to grimace. I should have let Zinnia heal me more. I hadn't realized how stiff and sore I'd be, but I sure as hell wasn't going to let them take me to see the healer. "See. Nothing that a few days of rest can't fix."

Payne narrowed his amethyst eyes. "You need at least a long soak in a healing pool."

"Except you're not using the pools." Lewin picked up the towel that I'd draped over the sink yesterday morning to dry. "Are you?"

"Why aren't you using the po—?" Payne started but his eyes flashed wide then narrowed with realization. "It isn't safe."

"I wouldn't know." I sagged back onto the bed. "I didn't want to find out."

"Probably for the best," Kit said as my stomach growled.

"All right. That's it," Grefin huffed as he shoved Lewin and Payne deeper into the room, crowding Kit against the wall by the window. He grabbed my arm and hauled me to my feet. "We're getting breakfast."

But Lewin blocked Grefin from dragging me out of my room. "Not smelling like that. I won't be able to keep anything down."

"You've eaten covered in shadow bear guts," Grefin said.

"Only because I was starving." Lewin opened my trunk and pulled out my second pair of pants and shirt. "Change first."

I took the offered clothes... and no one moved.

Swell.

With the four men crowded into the narrow space, the only place for me to change would be to stand on my bed, but there was no way I was taking off my heavy jerkin, let alone my shirt, in front of them.

"Not sure there's enough room to change my mind, let alone my clothes," I huffed.

Payne barked a sharp laugh, his eyes bright with surprise. "You better be out in a moment."

"How about I meet you in the great hall?" I suggested.

"Not happening." Kit nudged Grefin, who bumped Lewin, who pushed Payne out the door into the hall. "In your condition you could fall down the stairs."

"He's a guardsman," Grefin groaned as he tripped over Lewin's heels on his way out the door. "Pretty sure he can manage a few stairs."

"Depends if there's anyone else around," Payne grumbled, but he moved farther into the hall so Kit could step out of my room.

I shut the door and pressed my back against it even though my body weight wouldn't stop Payne if he wanted to get back in.

A smile tugged at my lips and I stared at the gray sky out my tiny window. It was difficult to tell what time of day it was in the gray, but given how bright it was — and how it had been morning in the Garden when Aster had removed the bracelet — it had to be full morning now.

Which meant, since Kit's team was on a night shift, that they'd just finished their shift and decided to check on me.

I didn't want to be happy about that. I was supposed to keep to myself so no one would ask questions and I could be a boy for as long as possible. And yet, after everything that had happened, it felt good that someone cared.

A small part of me wanted those caring someones to be Lords Rider, Quill, and Talon, but the rest of me, the smart part of me, knew that would only bring trouble. What little relationship I had with them was already too complicated.

With Kit, Payne, Lewin, and Grefin, I just needed to be Sawyer. I didn't also have to pretend I was fae or that I didn't already know them or everything else I needed to keep in mind when I was around Lords Rider, Quill, and Talon.

And I wasn't going to think about how my time in the Garden had suddenly become more complicated with Sir West, the spirit link, the High Priestess's plans and—

"Why are we waiting?" Grefin asked from out in the hall, reminding me that I couldn't just stand there.

If I didn't get moving, Payne was going to open my bedroom door and catch me with my shirt off.

I shrugged out of my jerkin and pulled off my shirt. The strips of fabric that I'd ripped from my dress when Sawyer and I had fled Herstind March were loose, and I quickly retied them then pulled on my clean shirt. After that, I dampened a small cloth and wiped myself down.

Lord Quill might have washed me in the Garden, but washing my spirit didn't translate into washing my body. Just like Zinnia had said that healing my spirit form didn't completely heal my physical form.

I kept the wipe down quick: to just my face, under my arms, and my hands. It didn't make me feel clean

— I'd have to do a more thorough washing for that — but hopefully it helped with the smell.

I changed my pants, making sure my belt with my sword was tight enough they wouldn't fall down, but loose enough so I could draw my weapon when I put on my slightly-too-big jerkin. Not that I anticipated I'd need to draw my weapon, but a guardsman was always prepared.

And changing my clothes, even if it was into identical clothes to what I always wore, reminded me of my purpose.

Here I was Sawyer Herstind, a man and a member of the Black Guard.

No one would protect me and I had to be careful to make sure I was never alone with Durand and Mikel, and probably the others in their group. But I also didn't have to demure to every man and I had two days of freedom. Or at least relative freedom since there was magic binding me to the Black Tower and I couldn't leave without permission.

Lord Rider had said I couldn't go to Lehyrst on my lieu time, but I didn't really want to. All the other novices were there to sleep with the pleasure house girls and do whatever else there was to do in Lehyrst. I was safer if I stayed where I was. All I really wanted to do was rest my aching muscles so I could survive whatever duties I was given in the next rotation.

And I had no doubt, after threatening to murder

Mikel, Durand, Hamlin, and Bramwell, and breaking Ambrose's nose, I was going to be on another, labor-intensive duty once my lieu days were done. Probably laundry duty.

Doing the laundry was just as hard as mucking out the stables. Although with the fae's soap — and the fact all the guards' uniforms were black — probably not nearly as smelly since I doubted we'd be using lye to clean things.

"Come on, already," Grefin called as he banged on the door.

I tossed my dirty shirt and pants in the sink to wash later and limped as fast as I could with my sore muscles into the hall.

"So here's your reminder," Lewin said as he tossed a heavy arm across my shoulders. "Sometime today go to the Quartermaster and get clean bedding and clothes. You can toss your dirty stuff in the laundry bin." He pointed to the narrow door beside the stair-well where the laundry bin was tucked away. "Don't bother dragging it all the way to the Quartermaster's office."

"Or better yet, drag it there," Grefin said as we walked past the seating area in the intersection between halls that was currently empty because it was the middle of the morning. "You're probably on laundry duty next and will be hauling it there anyway."

"Rider wouldn't be so cruel," Kit said, opening the

small side door just before we reached the large wooden doors at the end of the hall and ushering me and Lewin into the stairwell first. "You've done a full rotation plus extra time on stable duty. He's smart enough to know your muscles need to heal. There's no point in putting you on another hard-labor duty while going through novice training."

I didn't doubt that Rider was smart, but I wasn't sure about Kit's logic. Threatening to murder someone was serious, and for all I knew running the trail until I threw up was just the beginning of my punishment.

If everyone thought I was a liability, it wouldn't matter what kind of training I received now or later, I wouldn't be partnered with anyone or put in a position where someone counted on me to survive.

Maybe getting the physically harder jobs was better. It would be easier to stay unnoticed and the other guardsmen would feel like I was getting my just punishment. If I took care of myself, I might be able to keep my identity a secret indefinitely.

Except I knew that wasn't going to happen. Mikel and Durand had to be planning their retribution for what I'd said to them. They were probably coming up with ways to make me lose my temper in front of Rider again hoping for an even harsher punishment than just running the trail until I collapsed.

"No point in worrying about it right now." Lewin released my shoulders and ruffled my hair before hurrying down the steps ahead of me. "The duty list will go up tomorrow at lunch. You'll find out then what our great Lord Commander has decided."

"Until then, you're to spend the next two days soaking in a healing pool and walking around so your joints don't stiffen up," Payne said.

We reached the bottom of the stairs and headed straight into the great hall. It wasn't an assigned meal-time, so the hall was strangely quiet with only a few men sitting at the long tables. The crackling from the fires in the large hearths on either side of the room was loud, the sound sharp and snapping, echoing up to the vaulted ceiling, while light shone through the windows, brighter than usual, making me wonder if the sun was actually out or if the mist was just thinner today.

Grefin walked straight to the kitchen and the others followed. I hung back, trying to put space between us so the kitchen staff wouldn't think I was with them, but Kit grabbed my arm and tugged me in after him as if he didn't care if the kitchen staff thought he was a traitor by associating with me or not.

Inside, the fully armed guardsmen prepped lunch and washed dishes and pots. Large chunks of meat turned on spits over the one cooking fire, while steam curled up from enormous pots that hung over the other.

Half the men working in the kitchen looked up,

saw us, then turned back to what they were doing, the other half didn't bother looking up from their work at all.

"You're late. I was starting to get worried." The heavyset head cook set down his knife, grabbed a medium-sized pot and ladled stew from one of the enormous pots over the fire into it.

"Is that venison?" Lewin asked as he grabbed a tray from the stack of trays at the front of the counter and a bowl.

"Yep. Came in this morning," the head cook said as he brought the medium-sized pot over. "Figured you'd want this instead of porridge."

"If I wasn't already in love with Vreni—" Lewin flashed the man a brilliant smile and ladled a large helping into his bowl then moved down the line toward the bread.

The others grabbed trays and bowls and moved down the counter. Kit placed a bowl on my tray and nudged me ahead of him. When we reached the head cook, he gave Kit a nod, then turned away, not even glancing at me.

Kit ladled stew into my bowl, I grabbed a slice of bread and moved down the counter to the fruit. All the bowls were full with apples, pears, grapes, and even oranges.

I glanced at the men in the kitchen. No one watched me. They must have forgotten to hide the fruit when I'd stepped up to the counter... or they didn't want Kit and his team to know that they'd used my love of oranges to remind me of my place.

My fingers itched to take one.

The other guardsmen were going to push me around whether I took one or not.

And yet, I'd encouraged the rumor that I was getting special treatment so Mikel and his group would come after me because I needed to be a better fighter. I'd foreseen my death and, after being attacked by Mikel's group and Wells and Crane I knew I wasn't ready at all.

I swallowed back a bitter laugh.

If I was going to die tomorrow, I was having an orange. To hell with what the other guardsmen thought.

CHAPTER 32

Sage

I GRABBED an orange and limped out of the kitchen. Thankfully Grefin, Lewin, and Payne sat at the closest table, and I sagged onto the bench beside the enormous fae warrior.

"So when we're done eating, you're coming back to our rooms to soak in our tub," Kit said as he sat beside me, boxing me in with his mate. "The bathing salts aren't as good as the water in an actual healing pool, but it's better than a regular soak."

"And way better than the nothing you'd get in your room," Lewin added.

"In fact, why don't you move into the suite? We've got an extra room." Payne ate a mouthful of stew and groaned in pleasure. "Goddess, that's good."

"You can't move him into your suite," Grefin huffed. "Rider will assign you a permanent fourth soon."

"Not until after the competition." Lewin ripped off a chunk of bread and dipped it in his stew. "That's at least a few rotations away. Then there are the rotations to train for the White and Gold Towers and the competition rotations. By the time we have a fourth, the runt here will have had a growth spurt and will probably be our fourth. Besides, Payne isn't even using his room. We've got two empty beds just ready and waiting."

"He won't beat an experienced guardsman for an elite spot," Grefin huffed. "You think you're good enough, runt?"

I shoveled a spoonful of stew into my mouth, and salty, savory flavor exploded across my tongue. Payne was right. The stew was amazing.

Grefin was also right. I couldn't win the competition for an elite position in the guard, and I shouldn't even try. I had to keep my secret. Although I did need to become a better fighter if I was going to survive what was coming.

I picked up my slice of bread, the simple movement making my arms ache.

Maybe I should take Kit up on the offer to soak in the tub in their suite. It would be safer than using one of the pools in the basement. I might be able to sneak into the healing pool in the basement in the middle of the night, but there was still a chance someone would wander in... like Talon.

A shiver rolled through me at the memory of walking in on him in that pool when I'd first arrived.

Except there was still a chance Kit, Payne, or Lewin would walk in on me while I bathed. Sure, they were going to bed after this, but that didn't mean one of them couldn't wake up and need to piss. Would they knock, or would they walk right in?

I couldn't risk it.

"Unless *you're* entering the competition to be our fourth," Kit said to Grefin.

Grefin shrugged, his spoon halfway to his mouth. "Maybe I will."

"You did great taking down that bear the other night," Payne said.

Grefin huffed. "You and I both know I wouldn't have been able to finish it without your help."

"And that's why we're a team." Kit swiped his bread against the bottom of his now-empty stew bowl, sopping up every morsel of delicious gravy.

"Here's hoping we'll need a little teamwork tonight," Grefin said.

"Here's hoping." Lewin sighed. "I just about fell asleep last night in the saddle. I can't believe we didn't find anything."

"Maybe the shadows are finally figuring out that they need to stay away from the Tower, the Gates, and the ring," Payne said.

"Maybe we're finally putting a dent in their numbers," Grefin added.

That *would* be good. The shadow monsters didn't belong in the Gray. They belonged in the shadow realm on the other side of the Shadow Gate. Life in the Black Guard would become so much safer once all the monsters were gone. Then the job would be a matter of monitoring the Shadow Gate to ensure it stayed closed.

But the Shadow Gate had been magically sealed almost five hundred years ago and the Black Guard was still hunting shadow monsters. Was it really possible that we were finally winning the battle against the monsters?

"And maybe we just had a quiet night." Kit leaned back and stretched. "We're out again for two more nights and then we get lieu time. Let's not get sloppy now."

"I know you're just saying that for the runt's sake." Grefin drained his ale mug and stood. "You're the least sloppy team I know. You lost Hodge because that's the job sometimes, not because you're bad hunters. Everyone wants to be your fourth."

Lewin chuckled. "Guess you're actually going to have to work for something for once if you want to make this permanent."

"Guess I will," Grefin shot back.

The two men grabbed their empty trays and carried them to the bin where we were supposed to put our dirty dishes. Payne shoved the remaining large chunk of bread into his mouth and stood as well.

"So you're coming back to soak in our tub," Kit said as he picked up his own tray.

"I think I'll be all right." And I had to hope that was true.

While I desperately wanted a long soak in a tub with healing salts, I desperately wanted to keep my secret more.

Kit narrowed his eyes, clearly not believing that I'd be fine.

"We have dinner at the eight bell." Payne grabbed my tray and piled it on top of his. "Eat with us before we go out."

"Ah, sure."

I rescued my orange before Payne took my tray to the bin then watched the guys leave the great hall, Grefin to his room in the right wing and the others to their hunter team's suite in the left wing.

Now alone, I wasn't sure what to do.

I wanted to go back to my room and rest, but I wasn't ready to go back to the Garden — where I'd inevitably end up if I fell asleep. I was also afraid of how stiff I'd be when I woke again.

Better to keep moving and keep my muscles loose, so I wandered out the side door to the cramped area between the three-story barracks and the one-story section of the building where I'd stopped after my very first breakfast in the Gray.

It felt weird not having anything to do. This was the first time since I could remember when I didn't have a chore or someone to attend to. Even before my father had died, I'd had lessons and responsibilities. There were always people around watching and helping.

My life had even been more or less the same for a few years after mother had married Edred, but even before she'd passed, I'd started getting more chores and fewer lessons. By the time she'd died, I was pretty much just another servant in Herstind Castle, and servants didn't get days off.

I leaned against the Tower's stone wall, peeled my orange, and watched the men in the large bailey go about their duties.

Two men I didn't recognize pushed wheelbarrows filled with soiled hay and manure out of the stables and across the hard-packed dirt yard to the side door.

It was strange to see someone else on stable duty, but if what everyone said was true, I'd be assigned a new chore tomorrow afternoon. Unless you really pissed off Lord Rider or the Seneschal — who was the man responsible for duty assignments — or you had a special skill, you never got the same chore twice in a row.

Unlike Kit, however, I wasn't going to assume my

next chore would be less physically demanding than mucking stalls.

I popped a slice of orange in my mouth and savored the tart sweetness.

My next assigned chore, however, was the least of my worries. How long did I have before the vision of my death came true?

Given my current condition, I didn't stand a chance of fighting back. And from the fact that it looked like I'd been beaten and stabbed to death in my vision, I was in for the fight of my life.

Sure, I might have actually improved while Mikel, Durand, and the others were tossing me into the stream every day. But when they'd ambushed me yesterday — Father had it only been yesterday! — they'd also proven I hadn't improved nearly enough to survive what was coming.

I needed to be stronger and faster. I needed to hone my abilities. But just the thought of training even the regular amount we were supposed to train as guardsmen novices made my body throb in agony.

I released a heavy breath and ate another slice of orange. It didn't matter what I wanted or thought I needed right now. I'd already been pushed past my breaking point. I couldn't push myself any farther. My body wasn't up for anything. I needed to let it heal and the only way for that to happen was to rest.

Except I couldn't shake the feeling that I needed to do something.

So much of my life right now was completely out of my control: I didn't know what my next duty assignment would be, I had no control in the Garden, Zinnia had told me about things I could expect and how I could behave, but given my experience with Wells and Crane, I wasn't sure I completely believed her, and I sure as hell didn't know if Mikel and his gang were plotting my next punishment.

I huffed a bitter laugh. Of course they were. They were enjoying themselves in Lehyrst and figuring out what to do to me next.

I finished my orange and stiffly wandered out to the practice yard. I stared at the jagged gray landscape. There was less mist than usual and if I stared long enough, I managed to catch a weak, hazy glimpse of the sun.

Thirty men worked in the practice yard, twenty of them going through sword drills to keep in shape and improve their fighting abilities while ten practiced their archery.

Once we finished novice training, we'd be put into the standard rotation where we'd have morning or afternoon chores, alternating with training or guard duty. Regular guardsmen didn't hunt shadow monsters, we patrolled the road to the fae ring, the area around the Black Tower and near the Shadow Gate, and stood watch on the Tower's walls. We made sure the merchants who supplied the guard were protected and that we were ready for a shadow attack that everyone prayed wouldn't come.

I didn't understand why service in the Black Guard had to be a life sentence for humans. Sure, it was dangerous protecting the Gray from the shadow monsters that roamed the rugged land, but being in any army was dangerous, and other armies didn't require their men to give up their families for them or to commit to a lifetime of service.

Of course, given the selfish nature of mankind, it wouldn't surprise me if conscription had been the only way to fill the Guard's ranks when the Shadow Gate had been sealed five hundred years ago and the fae and human leaders had agreed to station a fighting force in the Gray.

But if the Black Guard only required a twenty-year service and people knew about the regular pay and the good food and lodging, I doubted the Five Great Kingdoms of Man would need to resort to the lottery to fill the Guard's ranks. The kingdoms and the lords would have to improve how they treated their own soldiers instead.

I watched two men join the others with their sword training. A few joked about them working on their lieu days, but the two men replied that they wanted a spot on an elite team and were getting ready for the competition.

For a moment, I wondered what it would be like to join the comradery and be lightly teased about wanting to practice instead of visiting one of the girls in Lehyrst. But even if I could physically handle training right now, I wouldn't be welcome. I wasn't sure if I'd ever be welcome.

Which was a foolish thought. I couldn't be welcome because I was a girl. I wasn't one of them and eventually I'd be found out. As much as it stung, not being welcome was one of the things protecting me.

I walked the perimeter of the practice yard to help my aching body and even contemplated walking the running trail for something to do.

But the thought made my stomach churn with a mix of the fear I'd felt when Durand and the others had attacked me, and the anger of running it over and over until I threw up.

The fourth bell rang, indicating lunch for those on the first shift, but since I hadn't eaten that long ago, I wasn't hungry. I also wasn't sure I wanted to brave the great hall all by myself.

I continued to do slow laps around the practice yard, giving the men who were training a wide berth, and let my mind wander. The fifth bell rang for the second shift's lunch and I watched men switch jobs, head back into the Tower or go to or from the practice yard. This was life at the Black Tower, and it felt strange to be standing on the outside watching and not doing anything.

I should go back to my room. I didn't know what to do, my mind kept sliding from one thought to the next without any real focus...

I was bored.

I huffed at myself. I couldn't afford to be bored. I had too much to worry about. On the tour of the Black Tower during my first official day as a guardsman, Talon had mentioned there was a library in the room above the great hall. If I couldn't help myself physically, I could still try to help myself mentally.

Maybe there was a book in the library that could help me understand why the fae's Garden thought my soul was fae and kept letting me in, or teach me about fae culture, or help me understand my magic. Hell, even having a better understanding of the shadow creatures and what I might face in the Gray while I pretended to be my brother would be helpful.

I went back up to the third floor and the large wooden doors at the end of the hall. Beyond them was an enormous room filled with towering bookshelves that were crammed with books and scrolls. Light poured from a large square in the center of the ceiling, and when I headed down the main aisle to look at it, I discovered it was a strange window that looked up at the sky. Given that the sky was gray and hazy, it was hard to tell how clear the glass was, but since it had to be a fae invention, I was sure the glass was perfectly clear.

The rest of the library was lit with bright fae lights, but while there were two main aisles — one running side to side, the other top to bottom — the rest of the shelves were organized into maze-like passages that reminded me a lot of the sacred grove in the Garden.

I glanced at the spine of the closest book, but it didn't have a title. The book beside it didn't have a title on the spine, either, and the one beside that had a title written in the fae's swirly writing.

I pulled out the first of the books that didn't have a title on the spine and opened it. It was a history of the Black Guard. The table of contents indicated that it covered the Guard's history for the first fifty years of its creation.

Interesting, but not necessarily useful for my various problems.

I put the book back and, with no idea where I was going and no one who I could ask, wandered down the first narrow aisle I came across.

The shelves had more history books both in the common human language and fae, some with actual titles on their spines. I reached an intersection, took the path on my right, and rounded a corner, stepping into a small reading nook.

The nook had two comfortable chairs on one side, a small desk and chair on the other, and a stunned Tyon holding a stack of books in the middle.

"It's ah... it's not what it looks like," the heavyset young man stammered.

CHAPTER 33
Sage

TYON'S WORDS SHOCKED ME, not because it looked like he wanted to make an excuse for whatever he was doing, but because he'd actually said something to me.

A part of me wanted to believe it was because he didn't recognize me, but I was the only person in the Black Tower with bright red hair and it was impossible not to recognize me.

The rest of me was just relieved I'd stumbled across Tyon in the nearly empty library. I shuddered to think what would have happened if I'd run across Durand or Mikel.

Tyon was around my real age of twenty and had spent the rotation running the trail at the end of each class with the bag of rocks. He had shaggy dark brown hair that needed to be trimmed out of his warm brown eyes and a round face that had probably been cheerful before his name had been drawn from the lottery.

I'd used him by suggesting he make friends with Talon and Quill to get special treatment. From what I'd seen, he hadn't tried to be friends with the captains, but he'd clearly passed on what I'd said, and I'd gotten way more than I'd bargained for with Mikel and his gang.

"I-I don't know where the dirty books are," he stammered.

"The dirty—?" What was he talking about?

"You know. The books with the pictures of naked girls." His cheeks turned bright red. "That's why you're here, right? Because you can't go to Lehyrst."

He thought I wanted to look at—? Because I couldn't leave the Gray and have sex?

My cheeks heated as well, probably turning the same shade as Tyon's. "No, I—"

What did I say to that? Were there actually books like that in this library? Given that Tyon and I were the only ones here, I suspected the books were a tale to trick the sacrifices.

"If you're not here for the books, why are you here?" I asked. Best to change the conversation and not have to come up with a masculine sounding answer to the dirty book question.

The blush swept across Tyon's forehead and down his neck. "To be a better reader," he mumbled.

I dropped my gaze to the stack of books in his hands. The top one was thin, and I recognized it as one of the early reading books my mother had used to teach me how to read. The next books weren't marked on the spine, but the last book was a dictionary.

"You're teaching yourself to read?"

I was seriously impressed. I wasn't sure how the dictionary would help if he couldn't read all the words, but it certainly showed his determination.

Tyon hugged the books to his chest. "I can read a little, but I want to get better."

"You don't really need to read to be a guardsman." All he really needed was to be able to read his name and the shift assignment sheet that was posted outside the quartermaster's rooms, and I was certain that was as much as half — probably more — of the Black Guard could manage. "I'm sure once we're done novice training, you'll be stationed in the kitchens."

I hadn't seen him in the kitchen during our first rotation, but he'd been an apprentice chef before his name had been drawn in the lottery. The head cook was probably thrilled at the idea of having another skilled set of hands in his kitchen.

"I'd rather go back to work for the Seneschal."

"Was that your chore last rotation?"

"I just did grunt work, running messages and clean and stuff," he said, "but I could have done so much more if I'd been better at reading."

"Would you like me—?" I waved at the books clutched to his chest, wanting to help him learn.

I hadn't been great at book learning and had needed Sawyer to help me, but Tyon looked so determined and hopeful.

And hope was what all the novices needed to find if they were going to survive as members of the Black Guard. With the exception of those who'd been raised knowing they were going to spend their life in the Guard, all the other novices thought their lives were now over.

The question was, would he want my help? He hadn't treated me badly like some of the other novices and guardsmen, but, like everyone else, he hadn't tried to help me, either.

And while I couldn't afford to make a lot of friends, there didn't have to be animosity between us.

Except Tyon was too shy and uncertain, too low in status to stand up against the others and make a gesture of peace toward me. I was going to have to take the first step.

"I can help if you'd like," I offered.

He glanced down at the books then around the room as if to confirm there was no one around — because associating with me was potentially dangerous.

"You won't tell anyone?" he asked.

"Who would I tell?"

"You're friendly with Talon and Lord Quill," he shot back. "And those other fae."

"Kit and Payne?" More like they'd decided they were going to take care of me, and I didn't have a say in the matter — for which, if I was being honest with myself, I was grateful. "I won't tell them, and I wouldn't say I'm friendly with Talon or Lord Quill."

Tyon's expression darkened. "I was surprised they left you there." He swallowed and inched a step away from me. "But you did threaten to kill Mikel and the others in front of everyone."

And I doubted that ingratiated me to the guardsmen. I'd probably just made my situation worse. They already thought I was a selfish nobleman because I'd come through the gate after dark. Mikel and the others had gotten away with ambushing me at the log bridge on the running trail because everyone thought Lord Rider's punishment to clean the stables hadn't been enough.

If I'd been thinking, I shouldn't have said anything. Or I should have at least waited until Rider wasn't in earshot. I'd just been so angry.

Father, it had felt so good to break Ambrose's nose.

Even just thinking about that crunch and the look on his and everyone else's faces made me smile.

Except I didn't know if my threat had worked, or if Durand and the others were going to be more aggressive when they came after me.

And all I could do now was stay alert and pray I could handle whatever they threw at me next.

"N-not that they didn't deserve it," Tyon added, his gaze landing on my bruised cheek. "Ambrose must have hit you hard. I'm surprised the swelling hasn't reached your eye."

I brushed my fingers over my tender cheek. There wasn't a mirror in my room or anywhere else that was easy to get to so I hadn't tried to see how bad the bruise was, but given how it felt — and everyone else's reaction to it — it had to look nasty.

"Listen," I said. "You've been kind enough to leave me alone. I'd like to repay you by helping you learn. But if it's going to bring you trouble, I'll turn around right now and forget we had this conversation."

"And if I say yes?"

"It can be a one-time deal today, or more, but if anyone else is around, you can pretend you don't know me."

I wasn't sure why I made the offer. Maybe because if I walked out of the library, I had no idea what I was going to do for the rest of the day. Or maybe it was because I needed to feel useful, and helping Tyon learn to read was an easy way to earn that feeling.

I'd been fleeing and fighting and praying since Sawyer's name had been drawn in the lottery, both in the Gray and the Garden. Spending a little time with

Tyon, doing something I knew I could do, made me think maybe I wasn't a complete disaster.

"All right," he said as he set the books on the desk and pulled the two comfortable chairs closer together.

I picked up the early reader and sat in one of the comfortable chairs and opened it to the first page. "Have you read this book before?"

"My master in the kitchen had shown it to me." He sat in the other chair and I placed the book on the chair arms between us. "I was apprenticed in a noble's house, and the tutor had left it on a table in the kitchen."

I brushed my fingers over the worn, vellum page. This was a collection of ten simple tales, stories most commoners knew already by heart. Minstrels often performed the tales through dramatic recitation or song but the words didn't vary much making it easier for those learning to read to recognize the words.

"My favorite tale is the one about the fae princess," he said.

"Then let's start with that." I flipped to the middle of the book and encouraged him to read the first word.

I help Tyon read through the fae princess story and then the next story and the story after that. We were halfway through the fourth tale of adventure when the eighth bell rang, the gong loud in the quiet library.

Tyon jerked upright in his chair. "The eighth bell already?"

I straightened as well and my body screamed in complaint, forcing me to swallow a groan. I shouldn't have sat for so long.

"I ah— I have to go." Tyon gathered his books and hurried away without a second look in my direction.

I wasn't sure if he was going to return them where he found them or if there was a librarian's desk where he could set them for the librarian to return them to their rightful place. I'd been listening and hadn't heard anyone else in the library, but that didn't mean there wasn't someone who kept the room tidy and the shelves in order.

I eased to the edge of the chair, thankful that Tyon had left so quickly. The fewer people who saw and heard me try to stand, the better. There was no telling if my current weakened state would be used against me.

I huffed a bitter laugh. Who was I kidding? If the wrong person saw, of course they'd use my weakened state against me.

Every muscle in my body ached, having stiffened up from sitting for too long, and I was trembling by the time I'd managed to stand. I hobbled around the small seating area, hoping to loosen up.

I'd promised Kit, Payne, and Lewin that I'd have dinner with them, and I didn't want them seeing me so stiff, but it was going to take more than a few laps around the tiny space for me to move normally, and I was sure Payne would send out a search party if I didn't show up.

Ugh. I should have taken the risk of being discovered and soaked in their tub while they slept.

CHAPTER 34
Sage

I HOBBLED two more laps around the small sitting area then headed down to the great hall. There I grabbed a plate with a thick slice of pork, mashed potatoes, and green and yellow beans, covered in gravy, a cup of ale, and another orange.

A small part of me cringed when the man behind me in line saw me set the fruit on my tray, but he didn't say anything and I reminded myself that they were going to punish me whether I had an orange or not, so I might as well have the treat.

Unlike the previous meals, no one tried to trip me when I left the kitchen, and thankfully Kit, Payne, and Lewin once again sat at a nearby table and I didn't have to walk the length of the great hall to get to them.

"Wow, you look almost as bad as when we woke

you," Lewin said as he shifted over on the long wooden bench to make room for me.

I set my tray on the table and sagged onto the seat, trying — and from Kit and Payne's expressions failing — to hide my wince.

"You went back to sleep, didn't you?" Payne said with a chuckle. "Big mistake."

"Yeah." I cut a slice of the pork on my plate and shoved it into my mouth. I didn't want to lie to them, but I'd promised Tyon I wouldn't tell anyone about his reading lesson.

"You should have soaked first." Kit nudged me with his elbow, making me look at him. "Will you take me up on my offer now?"

I glanced at the man at the table behind us. He wasn't too close, but he was eating alone and could easily concentrate on our conversation.

And while I didn't care what he thought about me, I did care that I might be making Kit and his team look bad. It was bad enough we were eating together. I didn't want to think about how the other guardsmen would treat them if it came out they were giving me special treatment.

At this point I didn't care how they treated me, but I did care about how Kit and his team were treated since Lewin was stuck in the Black Guard for life and Kit and Payne had to commit to fifty years.

I, on the other hand, was going to be thrown in a dungeon, returned to Edred, or killed, hopefully after five rotations.

Thankfully, it was just the one man I had to worry about within hearing distance. The eighth bell was the smaller second shift's evening meal bell and the night shift's breakfast bell. So while there were more men in the great hall than there'd been when we'd come down for breakfast, it wasn't nearly as packed as it was during regular meal time.

"You shouldn't be thinking about it for this long," Payne huffed.

Lewin chuckled and pointed his fork at the man behind us. "Don't worry about anyone else. We can handle them."

Grefin strolled up to the table and sat beside Payne. "Still trying to convince the runt to use your tub?"

"Don't know why," Lewin grumbled. "It's a perfectly good tub."

Grefin rolled his eyes. "If he wants to be an idiot, let him be an idiot."

"He's being an idiot because he thinks he needs to protect us." Payne shot me a hard look before taking a long swig of his ale.

"He's not being an idiot," Kit said "He's trying to be considerate. What he needs to know is that we don't care what the rest of the Guard thinks. We're a hunting team. An elite team, and we make sure it's safer for daytime patrols."

"Yeah," Lewin added. "They'd be fools to mess with us. We make their job easier."

"I'm pretty sure we got some fools in this year's novices," Grefin said with a pointed look at me.

And really, the guys were right. I'd be a fool to turn down a soak in their tub, especially while they were out hunting. There wouldn't be a chance that any of them would accidentally wander in on me, and I was already regretting turning them down in the first place.

If they said the other guardsmen weren't going to give them a difficult time about associating with me, then I needed to take them at their words.

I glanced at the man within earshot. Two other men had joined him and they were laughing about something.

In fact, it didn't feel like anyone except Kit, Payne, Lewin, and Grefin were paying attention to me.

Before, when I'd had my meals in the great hall with the guys, it had felt like everyone was watching me. It was probably because this wasn't a proper meal-time for most of the guard and there were fewer men in the room. I was sure things would go back to normal once my lieu time was over and I was back on a regular schedule.

The guys talked and joked about their upcoming

hunt and their plans for their lieu time in two days. I ate and listened and enjoyed the sense of camaraderie. Even if I wasn't really one of the men since I was still a novice and the Tower's most despised guardsman, it felt good to be included. If I hadn't been a woman, I would have enjoyed being part of their brotherhood.

Father, I wanted to be a part of it.

But being discovered was inevitable and dreaming about what I couldn't have would only make it hurt more.

The ninth bell rang and Kit grabbed my tray, stacked it on his, and took them to the bin for the dirty dishes.

"I'll meet you at the stables," he said to the others. "I want to show Sawyer to our suite."

"I'll have your horse saddled and ready for you," Payne said.

"Come on." Kit jerked his chin toward the door on the far side of the great hall, the one that led to the quartermaster's rooms, the infirmary, the elite team suites, and the individual suites for those of higher rank than a regular grunt like the quartermaster and the head cook.

There hadn't been a lot of reason for me to go into the Tower's right wing, so it felt strange to follow Kit into a narrow staircase, climb to the second floor, and head through a maze of halls to a plain wooden door.

Kit opened the door and placed his hand on the fae light just inside, illuminating a long, narrow utilitarian sitting room. There was a conversation area with a plain couch and two chairs by an empty hearth on the right side of the room, and a sturdy wooden table with four wooden chairs on the left. Two ale mugs and a small ceramic pitcher held open a map on the table, and a shirt and a sewing kit took up one of the seats on the couch.

At the back of the room, placed equal distance apart along the back wall, were five doors, two of the five were partially open letting in a little light from unshuttered windows.

"The bathing room is this one," Kit said as he walked to the first door on the right and opened it. "This room is empty if you want to stay the night."

He opened the door beside it revealing a simple bedroom like mine in the barracks. The only difference was this room was a little bigger and didn't have a sink... because, of course, the resident of this room had access to a private bathing room and didn't need his own sink.

The bathing room was about the size of the bedroom with a sink, tub, a set of shelves with towels and jars on it, and a small room in the front corner just big enough for an indoor privy.

The tub was larger than I expected, but given that half of an elite team had to be fae and fae men were bigger than human men, it made sense for a bigger tub. It also wouldn't surprise me if those who'd designed the tubs had anticipated that the men would want to soak their aching muscles instead of hiking all the way to the Tower's other wing to use the basement bathing house, and had made sure the tubs would be big enough for that.

"The salts are up here," Kit said, grabbing a large jar from the top shelf and moving it to a lower shelf. "You're supposed to use a handful." His attention dropped to my hands. "You should probably use two. Your hands are small and from how you've been walking, your aches are large."

I rolled my eyes at him. "That was a Payne joke."

"It very much was," he chuckled, and I smiled back at him. "All right. I have to go but make yourself at home and seriously think about staying the night."

He raised his eyebrows in a knowing look. I'd be safest in their suite.

Or at least I'd be safest in their suite for tonight since no one would know where I was. But the moment someone found out, I'd be just as safe in their suite alone as I'd be in my own room. And staying in my own room would draw less attention.

"I'll think about it," I told him as he hurried out the door. A door that also didn't have a lock.

I sighed and wandered over to one of the comfortable chairs by the cold hearth but thought twice about sitting. The chair was low to the ground and looked far too comfortable. Best to stay standing until I had my bath.

Except if I wanted to guarantee no one would walk in on me, I needed to make sure Kit and his team were well and truly hunting. Which meant I needed to wait.

CHAPTER 35

Sage

I HEADED to the table and studied the map. The Black Tower was marked in the top left corner, but it must have showed the side of the Tower opposite to the training grounds because I didn't recognize any of the landscape near the structure.

Someone had marked five X's in charcoal, but I didn't have any experience reading maps to tell what was marked or why.

And I was sure I'd only spent a few minutes looking at it. Not nearly enough time for Kit to get to the stables, saddle his horse, and the team to leave. Even if Payne had already saddled Kit's horse for him like he'd promised, the team was probably just leaving the bailey.

My gaze slid around the room looking for something to do and landed on the shirt and the sewing kit. I didn't know who needed to mend his clothes. I'd thought I was the only one who'd been punished by having to sew the rip in my pants and not been able to exchange it for a new one with the quartermaster. But maybe the rule applied even to elite teams.

Regardless, sewing was something I could do, especially if it was something as simple as rip, and it was an easy way to repay their kindness and make sure enough time had passed.

With that decided, I sat on the couch, found the rip, and carefully stitched it back together. Some of the buttons were also loose, so I reinforced those with a little more thread.

It had been dusk when I headed down for dinner and now there was no light coming through the partially open bedroom doors. Surely enough time had passed.

Groaning, I stood, shuffled to the bathing room, and turned the fae light as bright as it would go. Given how sore and tired I was, I didn't want to risk falling asleep. But I also knew I couldn't do a quick wash. If the healing salts were going to help, I needed to soak.

Just like with the sink in my room, there was a plug large enough to plug the drain at the bottom of the tub. I set it in place and turned on the taps then doled out a generous handful and a half of the salts.

While the tub filled with warm water, I undressed,

carefully setting out my clothes so I could jump out of the tub and redress as quickly as possible if necessary.

Not that my body would be happy with any quick movement, but I needed to be ready. If I listened carefully, I should be able to hear someone enter the sitting room, and I could only pray I'd have enough time to put something on before they opened the bathing room door. I wouldn't be able to bind my breasts, but I could at least get covered.

I set the strips from my old dress aside, so I could toss a towel on them if I needed to, and stepped into the warm water.

Oh, shadows!

I groaned half in pain and half in pleasure. It had only been a rotation and a day since I'd had a bath, but sinking into comforting warmth had never felt better.

I, however, had never looked worse. The bruise staining my side and chest had turned an ugly yellow green, but was also mottled with darker, newer bruises, and I had bruises on my thighs and arms from where I'd been struck with the practice blades.

If Sawyer could see me now, he'd be furious. But I also couldn't imagine Sawyer surviving half of what I'd already gone through. And that didn't count any of the *extra* training from Mikel and his gang.

Father, I hoped he was all right. He was still within the Five Great Kingdoms, possibly still in Erellod, but it was still summer and he had a horse. He wouldn't have to worry about bad weather or not being able to forage for food.

He could make it, and I would last long enough for him to do so.

I shifted and groaned, my aching muscles complaining with even that subtle movement.

I. Would. Last.

I sank a little deeper in the water, letting it lap at my lips and cheeks, and closed my eyes. I was determined not to fall asleep, but I also needed to relax or I'd waste the healing properties of the salts.

My thoughts drifted from where I thought Sawyer might be right now in his journey and how he was doing, to how I was going to handle Mikel and the others to what I was going to do when I finally let myself fall asleep and I returned to the Garden.

Something flickered at the edge of my sight and I heard a masculine yell. I jerked up but wasn't in the tub anymore. I stood in a forest clearing, the trees gnarled and twisted, growing out of a rugged rocky landscape. Fae light, hanging from a horse's saddle, danced around the clearing as the horse shied away from an enormous shadowy bear.

"Get back on your mount," Payne yelled as he slashed at the bear with one of his large swords and shoved a limp body toward the horse. "Get him to the Tower."

Grefin grabbed the body and the light flashed

across the injured man's face. It was Kit with a nasty gash down his cheek.

Someone screamed and Lewin staggered into sight clutching his leg. The bear roared and the horse reared back on its hindlegs. The fae light flashed in my eyes, sending light then darkness washing across my vision.

The scream came again, the sound wrenching at my soul. The guys were in trouble. I had to help, do something, save them.

"Hold him," someone barked. "We need to get this jerkin off him."

I blinked, clearing my vision, but now I stood in the infirmary, the bright fae light illuminating Kit and his team in horrific brilliance.

Kit writhed on a table, blood pouring from where his hand used to be onto the polished stone floor. His jerkin was torn open and more blood oozed from his chest. Two guardsmen helped cut away his jerkin and shirt, revealing the deep gashes in the fae's chest, while Flint placed his hands on the man and used his magic.

"Fuck," he said. "I need two drams of wistellel."

One of the guardsmen grabbed a rolling table with medical supplies and the other rushed to grab a jar from the medicine cabinet and pour it into a small cup.

"You have to save him," Payne moaned, and my vision jerked me around the room.

Lewin lay unconscious on the next table, his right thigh shredded down to the bone and a growing pool of blood forming beneath his torso, while Grefin sat in a chair, holding one towel to the side of his head and the other to his calf.

Payne leaned against the wall next to him, clutching a severed hand, his eyes blank and stunned and his complexion gray. "Save him. Save him," he hissed over and over. "You have to save him."

"He's losing too much blood." Flint hurried to Payne and grabbed the severed hand.

"Save him."

"Working on it," Flint hissed between clenched teeth as he brought the hand to bleeding stump.

He closed his eyes, his expression tight with concentration. The guardsmen who'd moved the rolling table closer started wrapped a bandage around the connection as if fae magic was all that was needed to reattach a hand.

And while that might have been the case, sweat beaded on Flint's forehead and his breathing grew heavier as if he were running the trail and not just standing there with his eyes closed.

Then Lewin screamed and his breathing turned short and sharp.

"Damn it." Flint turned away from Kit to take care of Lewin. "I need to stabilize him."

The man with the medicine rushed back to Kit and tried to get him to drink, while the other man cut away Kit's pants, revealing more injuries.

Father, he must have been mauled by that bear. It was a miracle he was still alive.

"I can't believe there were five of them," Grefin groaned. "How the fuck were there five of them?"

"Please," Payne said. "Save him."

"He needs to drink," the guardsman said.

But Kit screamed, the medicine dripped out of the side of his mouth, and he started to convulse. His foot slammed against the table, knocking it over with a crash and sending the medical equipment flying, and one of his arms caught the guardsman with the medicine in the face, sending him stumbling back.

Payne suddenly gasped. His eyes flashed wide and he clutched at his heart before dropping to the floor with a thump.

My pulse lurched.

No. Please no.

"Fucking hell." Flint leaped across the room and grabbed Payne's hand. "Shadow venom?" His gaze shot to Grefin. "I thought you said you fought bears, not serpents."

The guardsman who'd been trying to get Kit to drink, rushed back to the medicine cabinet, pulled out another jug, and started to pour.

"Stop," Flint said, and the vision wrenched my gaze back to Flint and Payne. "It's too late. We're seconds too late. It's already reached his heart."

I jerked up, sloshing water out of the tub, my chest tight with panic.

They were there.

Right now.

Everything within me screamed that at that very moment Flint was trying to save Kit and Lewin.

And Payne was going to die if I didn't do anything.

Oh, Father. I'd never been able to change one of my visions before. My father had died. My brother had died. And so had my mother.

I'd hoped when I'd taken Sawyer's place that I had changed things, but I had no way of knowing if I had, not until I knew for certain he was safe.

But this time—

Please.

I had to save Payne. I had to change what I'd seen. Tonight had to be the night I succeeded.

Don't miss the next book in the series!

Hidden Within the Secret Heart
Desperate Disguise: Book Four

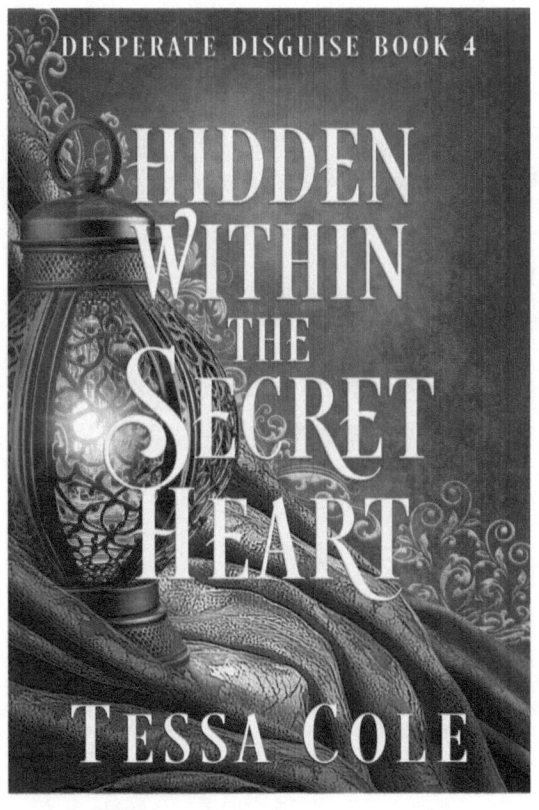

Other Books by Tessa Cole

DESPERATE DISGUISE

Lies Within the Darkest Tower, book 1

Stand Against the Rising Storm, book 2

Whispers Within the Midnight Garden, book 3

Hidden Within the Secret Heart, book 4

NEPHILIM'S DESTINY

Destined Shadows, prequel story

Destined Darkness, book 1

Destined Blood, book 2

Destined Fire, book 3

Destined Storm, book 4

Destined Radiance, book 5

ANGEL'S FATE

Fated Bonds, book 1

Fated Winter, book 2

Fated Fear, book 3

Fated Despair, book 4

Fated Resolve, book 5

Fated Heart, book 6

ENSNARED BY THE PACK

Wolf Deceived, book 1

Wolf Denied, book 2

Wolf Desired, book 3

Wolf Distressed, book 4

Wolf Decided, book 5

Wolf Devoted, book 6

THE GRECIAN GODDESS TRILOGY

Written with Clara Wils

Kiss of the Goddess, book 1

Power of the Goddess, book 2

Bonds of the Goddess, book 3

SECRETS GODS KEEP

Written with Clara Wils

Craving Demons, book 1

Chaos Demons, book 2

Claiming Demons, book 3

HER BAD BOY WOLVES

Written with Clara Wils

www.ingramcontent.com/pod-product-compliance
Lightning Source LLC
Chambersburg PA
CBHW031551240626
47153CB00002B/469